FAITH UNCHAINED

ESCAPING THE SNARE OF A
MISLEADING SPIRITUAL LEADER

LASHEA HUNTER

ISBN 978-1-962929-56-1

First Printing – November 2025
Proudly Printed in the United States of America

Digital Publishing Florida, Inc.
Oldsmar, FL 34677
Digitalpubfl.com

Table of Contents

Foreword

Faith Unchained by Apostle LaShea Hunter should not be regarded as a mere memoir, but as a testimony with the power to draw others into greater freedom. Her care and intent to be an agent of deliverance is palpable in even the grittiest details. By unpacking her moments of pain, shame, and contradiction, Apostle Hunter provides language for the uncomfortable and unexplainable stations one may encounter while trudging along the road to inner healing. With a relationship anchored in Yeshua (Jesus), there is hope to destroy every tight and heavy chain and recover His purpose for your life!

- Apostle LaTonya R. Hite
Senior Pastor, Bethel Revival Assemblies of America &
Founder, Lifeline Prayer Network
Emporia, Virginia

As a healthcare provider, I've witnessed the deep wounds that pain and trauma leave behind—wounds that medicine alone cannot heal. Faith Unchained speaks to those hidden places, to the very soul of religion and dysfunction. It gives the captive permission to speak their truth, to acknowledge the brokenness that comes from abuse, and to discover healing through the living Word of God.

This book is both redemptive and restorative. It offers wisdom, comfort, and practical resources for anyone who may still be walking through the shadows of spiritual or emotional pain.

I wholeheartedly recommend Faith Unchained to all who are in Christ and to those seeking to know Him. There is something within these pages for everyone—the broken, the offender, the victim, and even the healed. This is not just a book; it is a divine instrument of healing, reconciliation, and truth.

- Cory Forte, Family Nurse Practitioner — Lucama, NC

Prelude: The Silence Ends

I was sixteen when everything I thought I knew about love, family, and faith unraveled.

I didn't run away. I was rejected.

The ones called to protect me turned their backs. The place I called refuge—a church—became a prison of silence. And I lived in that silence for thirty-six years.

For decades, I was told to keep quiet, to protect the church's image, to forgive and forget. I obeyed that command in fear, not in faith. I wept in private, served without complaint, traveled and travailed—quietly. I stayed silent to preserve the name of a man who used God's name as a shield for manipulation.

But I can't stay silent any longer.

I do not write these words to accuse. I write to heal—for myself and every daughter of the faith who was made to believe that being chosen by God meant being abused in His name.

I didn't know I was walking into a trap.
But my mother did.

She saw what I couldn't. At sixteen, I thought I was chasing God, following the path of purpose. But I was really following a man with a past—one the whole town of Wilson, North Carolina, whispered about. I didn't hear those whispers. I was too eager for love, too hungry for belonging to ask the right questions.

The man who called himself my spiritual father had been to prison. Accused of abusing the children of the woman he later married. Still, I was blinded by what I thought was favor. Blinded by scripture twisted into chains. "Honor your father and mother in the Lord," he would preach. "But if they don't speak God's word, you're not obligated to obey."

I believed him.
I believed I was choosing righteousness.
I believed I was honoring God.
I believed my mother was rebellious.

Until the day I came home from church after midnight and found my clothes bagged up on the porch. A note was taped to the door. It read:

"If you're going to follow that ministry you can't stay here."

So I left. Not because I was rebellious—but because he had convinced me she was.

What followed was 36 years of silence.

36 years of control.

36 years of trauma dressed in titles.

I trusted him with my soul.

And he eventually took my body too.

————

Why I'm Finally Telling My Story

This book would never have been written if God hadn't come to me in a dream—through the very man who once broke me.

Apostle McKinney was the man I once called my father in the gospel. He was also the man who abused me. My abuser. My spiritual leader. My captor. The one I honored publicly while I bled privately.

He has since passed on—moved to heaven. Forgiven by God. And in His mercy, the Lord allowed him to visit me in a dream. Not to haunt me. Not to excuse his sins. But to deliver a message that would shift the course of my life and ministry.

In the dream, I was standing in the new home I had just started building, reviewing my decorating plans. Apostle McKinney walked in gently, no trace of shame or fear. Just presence. He looked around and said:

"You don't need any accessories. All you need is plants."

At first, I was confused. But as I prayed and sought God, He revealed:
Plants represented life, truth, authenticity. Not decoration. Not performance. Just what lives, grows, and breathes. Plants also clean the air and produce oxygen. Spiritually, my testimony and transparency will purify the "atmosphere" of my ministry, bringing life-breath to others who have been suffocated by secrecy, shame,

or abuse. I am being called to *cultivate*, not perform — to tend to souls like a gardener tends plants: patiently, intentionally, and with care.

My ministry will be marked not by quick "decorating" of people's lives, monitoring their outward appearances but by deep transformation and nurturing growth.

Then the dream shifted.
We were suddenly inside the funeral home that had handled his death and burial. The staff turned to me angrily and said, *"She dug him up."*

But God was showing me in essence that "Digging him up" means *refusing to let* the false narrative of what really happened remained buried.

- Spiritually, it was God showing me that part of my ministry will involve unearthing what others wanted to keep hidden — especially truths that challenge the image of a respected figure.
- People's *anger* represents the resistance, backlash, and misunderstanding that always comes when darkness is brought into the light (Ephesians 5:11).

But in the dream Apostle McKinney had no reaction.
He didn't speak to them—he spoke to me.
With a calm, heaven-borne authority, he said:

"LaShea, you can't build your ministry on lies. You must tell the truth of what happened to you. Don't hold your story to protect me any

longer. Your silence is not saving me. But your story will deliver oth-
ers."

I stood there in the dream, undone by his words.
For 36 years, I had buried my truth beneath his title. I protected his image, honored his ministry, and carried my pain like a secret vow. But the Lord used even my abuser—now healed and home in glory—to release me with divine permission:

Tell your story.

Because in my story are keys to somebody else's freedom.
Because my ministry is not built on shame or secrecy.
It is built on truth. And truth still sets people free.

I didn't want to expose another church scandal. I had already spent decades protecting the man who hurt me, afraid that my truth would damage the people who loved him, followed him, or still believed in him. I didn't want people to question God because of one man's failure. I didn't want to be one more person holding a match in the house of God, which is already smoldering with scandals— affairs, cover-ups and money laundering.

But silence doesn't heal.
It infects.
And what's infected in the body will eventually cause death if left untreated.

I'm not telling this story to bring down a man of God or tear apart the church.

I'm telling it to heal the church.

To restore the wounded.

To confront the sickness hiding behind pulpits, one heart at a time.

——

What This Book Is About

This is my testimony—raw, unpolished, and unchained.

I wrote this book for anyone who's ever questioned their own voice because a leader told them they couldn't hear from God without their affirmation. For every believer who stayed too long in a toxic church because they feared disobeying God. For every soul that mistook manipulation for mentorship.

I want to give language to the pain. To help others understand what spiritual abuse really looks like—especially in prophetic, charismatic circles where power can easily turn into control.

This book is a survival guide and a call to action.
It's an invitation to heal.
And it's proof that God still restores.

———

Chapter 1

What Does Faith Unchained Mean?

1. Faith That Breaks Free from Bondage

"It is for freedom that Christ has set us free..." — Galatians 5:1 (NIV)

This kind of faith refuses to stay trapped in fear, shame, or spiritual control. It breaks the chains people wrapped around your voice and your calling—even when they wore a robe while doing it.

2. Faith That Refuses to Stay Silent

"God has not given us a spirit of fear..." — 2 Timothy 1:7 (NKJV)

When you've been spiritually abused, your confidence in hearing from God can shatter. Faith Unchained is about regaining the boldness to trust Him again—for yourself. It's the courage to speak, even after you've been silenced.

3. Faith That's Raw, Real, and Restored

"After you have suffered a little while, the God of all grace... will restore, confirm, strengthen, and establish you." — 1 Peter 5:10 (ESV)

This isn't polished, platform faith. It's the gritty kind that's been through betrayal, grief, and fire—and came out forged, not forgotten.

4. Faith That Frees Others

"They overcame by the blood of the Lamb and the word of their testimony..." — Revelation 12:11 (NIV)

Unchained faith doesn't just set you free. It throws the keys to someone else. It declares: You can get out too.

5. Faith That Faces the Truth

"And you shall know the truth, and the truth shall make you free." — John 8:32 (KJV)

Truth is not the enemy. Cover-up is.

Faith Unchained means you can hold the truth and still hold on to God. You don't have to choose one or the other.

Who Are the Chained?

You'll find them in every pew, on every praise team, and even behind pulpits—faithful people bound by experiences they're too ashamed to name.

They are the Silenced Servant:
She pours herself out in church, but goes home numb. She's been told submission is holiness—even when it cost her her voice. She doesn't speak up, not because she agrees, but because she's afraid.

They are the Performing Prophet:
He has gifts, but he's grieving. He knows how to preach, pray, and prophesy, but no one knows the price of his private torment. He thinks his pain is the cost of the oil—so he never questions the system that wounded him.

They are the Manipulated Mentor:
She was trained to teach others, but taught under control. Her identity was shaped by someone else's agenda, so she doesn't know who she is outside of the structure. She doesn't trust herself to lead without asking permission.

They are the Shamed Daughter:
She once walked in purity, but got caught in the web of admiration and spiritual attention that turned possessive. She's now hiding in ministry roles, afraid to admit the confusion and shame she still carries.

They are the Confused Believer:
He wonders how a man of God could be so anointed and so abusive. He's still trying to reconcile the miracles with the manipulation, the laying on of hands with the hidden harm. He loves God—but doesn't know who to trust.

They are the Bound But Brilliant:
She knows she's called. She knows she's different. But she's been trained to play small. She's afraid that if she ever truly shows up in her God-given identity, she'll be seen as rebellious, disobedient, or "too much."

——

Why They Need to Be Unchained

Because God never asked us to stay loyal to what is killing us.

Because love doesn't control, confuse, or crush your calling.

Because faith is not about pretending—it's about trusting God enough to confront the lies, the silence, and the systems that are not like Him.

Faith Unchained is for every person who looked up to someone they thought was godly—only to find themselves emotionally trapped, spiritually manipulated, and too afraid to leave.

It's time to say:

> "*This is not what Jesus looks like.*"
> "*This is not my final chapter.*"
> "*This is not how my story ends.*"

I know what it means to be chained.

This isn't just spiritual talk—it was the lived reality of my life. I had a full scholarship to a university. I was accepted into a program with a focus on computer science and programming—at a time when the Information Age was just beginning to boom. I was on the edge of something historic, something great. I could feel it.

But he told me I could leave and I'd be successful…
"But when you reach the top, the bottom will fall out."

That one sentence frightened me just enough to stay. I trusted the prophet. I've always had a reverence for God.

I didn't know that fear dressed in prophecy is manipulation. I didn't know that you could be warned by someone spiritual but not truly protected. I didn't know that God never speaks in a way that contradicts His own plan to prosper you.

So I remained "faithful."
Faithful to his vision.

Faithful to his ministry.

Faithful to a man who wrapped my brilliance in bondage and called it loyalty.

If he went somewhere, I went with him.

If I had a desire to explore, to grow, to build something of my own—it was dismissed.

And if I acted outside of what pleased him, I was rebuked or made to feel as if I had sinned against God.

It was bondage.

And the part that cut the deepest?

Everyone thought it was mutual.

They assumed I was in agreement.

That I wanted to serve like that. That I was flattered, chosen, covered.

But I wasn't. I was a young girl who didn't know I had choices.

I was a daughter of God chained to the shadow of someone else's calling.

I was suffocating in silence, giving up my future to build his.

I didn't get to pursue the brilliance God placed in me.

I didn't get to become a great voice in technology or innovation.

I didn't get to expand and develop as a woman in society—because my whole life was orbiting someone else's "assignment."

And it wasn't God.

It was control.

It was fear.

It was spiritual abuse.

I was in bondage. And I want you to know: if you're there now, you are not crazy—and you are not alone.

Faith Unchained is the sound of keys rattling.

It's the sound of chains breaking.

It's the sound of a woman finding her way out… and throwing the door wide open for you too.

The Truth About Emancipated Faith

God never intended for our faith to be chained to people.

To places.

To personalities.

Or to platforms.

Our life of faith is meant to be emancipated—rooted in freedom, flourishing under grace, and guided by the voice of God Himself.

Yes, God gives us leaders.

Yes, God uses spiritual authority.

Yes, God places us under teaching and discipleship for seasons of growth and grounding.

But never for ownership.

The role of a spiritual leader is not to keep us dependent—it is to train us to be discerning.
It is to teach us how to hear from God for ourselves, to cultivate our own relationship with the Father, and to recognize His voice above every other.

Healthy leadership doesn't control. It releases.
It doesn't silence. It equips.
It doesn't demand loyalty to man—it builds devotion to Jesus.

Faith is never meant to be lived under a microscope of scrutiny, suspicion, or fear.
It's not a contract—it's a covenant.
It's not meant to be caged—it's meant to be walked out in full expression.

You should be able to discover your calling and pursue it—from your youth.
You should be allowed to develop it without guilt or pressure to trade your future for someone else's present.

And when the time comes, your leaders should bless you, release you, and celebrate you—not clip your wings to keep you close for their benefit.

You were not saved just to make a church great.
You were saved to *make disciples*—to multiply, to mentor, to move in what God has placed inside of you.

This is the kind of faith Jesus modeled:
He trained.
He imparted.
He sent.

He didn't keep the disciples tied to Himself. He gave them power, then sent them into the world.

That's what emancipated faith looks like.

And that's what we're reclaiming in these pages—freedom to follow God fully, boldly, and without apology.

Chapter 2

A Foundation of Prayer and Power: Divine Passion

When my mother left my stepfather, it was more than a breakup. It was an uprooting. We moved into a modest house near the fairgrounds on the outskirts of Wilson, North Carolina. On the surface, it was just another address. But to me, it felt like exile. We were now far from everything familiar—our extended family, our friends, and most painfully, my church.

The Wilson Revival Center had been more than just a place of worship to me—it was home. A spiritual womb. A launching pad. The place where I first heard the voice of God and began to discover who I was in Him. I remember begging God in prayer, "Lord, please don't let her get that house." I knew what that move would mean. My mother didn't drive, and I was too young to get myself around. No car meant no church, and no church meant no lifeline.

But despite my desperate pleas, the deal went through. The house became ours—and with it, a season of deep isolation. There were occasional rides from people to go to the churches my mother wanted to go to, but they weren't taking me back to where my soul had been fed. I tried to be gracious. I tried to adapt. But my heart wasn't in it. And slowly, like a fire left untended, my spiritual flame began to dim.

That summer, I wandered. I don't mean just physically—I mean spiritually. I drifted into places I never thought I'd go. Places where the voice of God felt faint, and my own voice grew louder. That was the summer I lost my virginity. The summer I backslid. The summer I tried to fill spiritual hunger with natural things, only to feel emptier than before.

One night, I found myself in a club. The music was deafening—so loud it felt like it was trying to drown out my conscience. Bodies pressed in on every side, people dancing, laughing, losing themselves in the moment. But I couldn't lose myself. Because in that moment, I was found.

It was as if heaven pulled back a veil, and for a brief second, I saw the spiritual reality of the room. It didn't look like fun—it looked like torment. I didn't see people enjoying themselves; I saw souls bound in invisible chains. I knew then that this wasn't my place. I didn't belong here. The air was thick, and not with smoke or perfume—but with SIN.

"I want to go home," I whispered to a friend. She arranged a ride for me, and when I climbed into the car, I noticed something reflecting in the glove compartment. Drugs.

My heart dropped.

I sat in the backseat, silent, my pulse racing. The weight of my decisions came crashing down on me all at once. "Lord," I whispered under my breath, "if You let me make it home safely, I promise—I promise I'll give You my heart, once and for all."

That night, I cried myself to sleep. But it wasn't the cry of a victim—it was the cry of a prodigal. I said to God with trembling sincerity, "I don't want an on-again, off-again relationship with You. I don't want to keep falling in and out. I want to be faithful. I want to be steady. I want to be Yours."

I didn't know it, but heaven had already heard me. The very next night, I was invited to a youth revival. The sermon? *"Let Us Return to the Lord."* The preacher read from Hosea and every word felt like it was aimed directly at my soul.

That night, I returned.

But this wasn't the emotional high I'd had before. This wasn't about goosebumps or another trip to the altar to cry and fall. No. This was different. This was a deep, seismic shift. I came back with a hunger I couldn't explain and a thirst that only His presence could quench.

I wasn't seeking a word from a prophet. I wasn't settling for just being a church goer. I just wanted God. The real God. The God behind the preaching and the platform. I wanted to know His Word, to understand His ways, to walk with Him the way Enoch did—daily, honestly, completely.

I remember night after night, curling up on the floor of my room with my Bible open and tears falling on the pages. I'd underline verses and ask the Holy Spirit, "What does this mean? What are You saying?" Sometimes I didn't hear anything. Other times, it was like He sat beside me and whispered revelation into my soul.

Church became more than a weekly gathering. It became oxygen. I didn't have a ride half the time, but I found ways to get there. If I had to walk, I walked. If I had to wait an hour for someone to pick me up, I waited. I didn't need encouragement - I just needed proximity. I wanted to be near the fire.

I began to serve—wherever I was needed. I sang in the choir. I helped with the youth. Directed the choir. Attended noon day prayer. I didn't care what it looked like. I wasn't trying to fit in, I was building a relationship with the King.

There were times when the presence of God would meet me so strongly in prayer, I would weep until I couldn't move. I remember one particular night, kneeling by my bed. I had been fasting—not for a blessing, but for clarity. I wanted to keep now what pleased the heart of God. As I began to pray, something shifted in the atmosphere. The room became thick with His glory. I felt like I was no longer on earth. My tongue changed. I began to pray in a heavenly language I had never spoken before. My body trembled—not from fear, but from glory. And in that moment, I heard the Lord say:

"I'm calling you to be a voice, not an echo. You will not repeat the systems of men. You will carry the sound of My Spirit. He said: You will be a reformer!"

I wrote it down and placed it under the mattress of my bed. I've never shared that with anyone until now.

That encounter sealed me. From then on, I prayed not just for breakthrough—I prayed for burden. *"Lord, give me Your heart,"* I'd cry. *"Let me feel what You feel."*

And He did.

I began to weep for the lost, for those without God, starving for relationship. Sometimes I would wake up in the middle of the night with names on my heart and pray until peace came. I started journaling those moments, writing down the things God whispered to me. That journal became a personal altar—a record of the whispers that built my calling; A young girl with a God impression for life!

Temptation still knocked. The enemy didn't give up on me. But this time, I wasn't fighting from a place of guilt—I was fighting from a place of grace. I had tasted the real. I had seen the beauty of holiness. I wasn't perfect, but I was changed.

And I was committed.

I began to understand that my passion for God wasn't just a phase. It was the evidence of a divine calling. My hunger wasn't just to be saved from sin. It was to be launched into purpose. I wasn't just escaping hell—I was being prepared to pull others out of it.

I didn't know everything then. But I knew enough to say yes.
I didn't come from a long line of preachers. I wasn't the daughter of a bishop or a mother in Zion. I was just a girl—a little brown girl with a broken home, a loud soul, and a heart that beat too fast when church music played.

I grew up in a house where God wasn't ignored, but He wasn't embraced either. Most of my family wasn't saved. My mother—was a believer but was a woman fighting depression and oppression, trying to raise three children while quietly unraveling beneath the weight of her own insecurities. She loved us, I know she did, but she often disappeared into her pain. When life became too much for her, she turned inward—and I turned upward.

From 10 to 16 years old, I was the one waking up early to cook meals for my younger siblings. I learned how to iron clothes and put babies to bed before I even knew how to truly spell "responsibility." Childhood slipped through my fingers while I played mother in a house missing its rhythm.

But even then, something deep inside me was awakening. It was more than survival. It was more than wanting relief. It was divine passion.

———

When the Spirit Found Me

One of the first times I ever felt the Spirit of God, I was standing in a little wooden church on the same street we lived on. The choir was singing something I didn't know the words to, but my heart knew the language. Something hit me so hard I didn't know if I was crying or breathing—or both.

It wasn't just emotion. It was encounter.
The presence of God fell on me like rain on dry ground. And for the first time, I felt seen.

I didn't know how to explain it to anyone, so I didn't. I just kept going back. I showed up to every service, whether I understood what was happening or not. I was just a girl sitting on the pews with a notebook, writing down scriptures I couldn't yet pronounce and songs I didn't know the verses to.

While other girls were dreaming of boyfriends and dances, I was asking God to make me His.
"Lord, I don't know why I feel like this. But whatever *this* is, I want more of it."

I Prayed Myself Into Belonging

At night, when the lights were off and the house was silent, I would slip onto the floor beside my bed. My knees would ache on the worn carpet, and I'd whisper prayers like secrets to the only One who listened without interruption.

"Jesus, can You hear me?"
"God, are You real like the preacher said?"
"If You're really my Father, can You help me not feel so alone?"

I was too young to know what intercession was, but I prayed like the world depended on it.
Because mine did.

I prayed over my siblings while they slept. I prayed over my mother, asking God to deliver her from sadness I didn't have language for. I prayed over myself, that I wouldn't grow up too fast or too bitter. That I wouldn't break beneath the weight of being needed but not nurtured.

And somehow, God met me there—in my little bedroom, with my white furniture and white canopy bed, with childlike faith talking to God, with my little child's voice and the audacity to believe He was listening.

The Fire that Marked Me

One Sunday, a visiting evangelist pointed at me during altar call. "You—yes, you! There's a mantle on your life," she shouted. "You'll preach to nations. But first, you must pray because you will encounter some things that will prepare you for your call!"

I trembled under the weight of the words. Me? A girl who didn't even own a Bible of her own yet?

But I took that word and folded it into the pages of my heart like a promise from heaven.
And I began to pray like the call had already come.

I prayed until my voice cracked.
I prayed until I saw things in dreams I didn't understand.
I prayed until I started hearing God's voice in whispers that shook me more than any sermon could.

God wasn't just visiting me—He was calling me.

I Belonged to God Before I Belonged Anywhere Else

I didn't have a family legacy of holiness. I didn't have a mother who could teach me the depths of the word of God. But I had a secret place. And in that place, God became my teacher, my father, my closest friend.

The world didn't know it, but a preacher was being formed in the back bedroom of a fragile little house.

I didn't understand the theology. I just understood the longing.
And God met me there—not because I was qualified, but because I was hungry.

That hunger became my compass. That prayer life became my lifeline.
And long before I stood behind pulpits or traveled to speak to people.
I was just a little girl praying in the dark,
Calling heaven to earth,
Believing I was born for more.

I didn't have the language for it then, but I was an adult long before I was grown.

My mother had suffered a nervous breakdown years earlier—a wound that never fully healed. She was never quite the same after that. Some days, she was present and laughing, cooking dinner and brushing my hair. But other days, she disappeared behind her eyes. Her voice would dim. Her body was there, but her mind had gone somewhere darker, somewhere I couldn't reach.

And that's when I'd step in.

I became her cushion. Her shield. Her replacement.
Not because I wanted to—but because I had to.

My baby sister Angel was just a baby. Ten years younger than me, she looked up at me with big brown eyes that trusted me like a second mother. My baby brother Bryan came a few years later, and together they both looked to me for structure, for safety, for something that felt like home.

I treated my siblings like they were my children. They trusted me and in most times, I was the only one they would be comforted by. Children know spirits. They understand love when no words are spoken. God granted me the ability to be a mother when I was just a girl.

I would wipe my mother's tears in the evening and help her hold herself together when the darkness crept back in. I didn't know how to fix her, but I knew how to cover her. And somehow, I believed that was enough.

My Childhood Was a Warzone of Silence and Strength

There were no family meetings. No explanations. Just the knowing.
The knowing that if I didn't do it, it wouldn't get done.
The knowing that if I broke down, we would all fall apart.

So I smiled when I needed to cry. I stayed strong when I wanted to scream. I carried groceries in my arms and burdens in my spirit.

I remember nights where I'd rock Angel to sleep, singing songs I made up just to drown out the sound of Mama crying in her room. Bryan would crawl beside me in the bed, and I'd pretend like everything was normal—like we were just playing house and not surviving it.

And even then, I prayed.

I'd sneak into the bathroom, run the shower water to mask the sound, and cry on the floor asking God to help me.
To help her.
To help us.

"God, why is she like this?"
"Why can't I just be a kid?"
"What if she doesn't come back from that place this time?"

I lived between fear and faith. Between grown-up responsibility and little-girl ache.

But even in that confusion, God was carving out a sanctuary in me.

———

How God Used That Pain to Train My Spirit

What I didn't know then—but I know now—is that God was developing my capacity before I even had language for destiny. That brokenness was my bootcamp. That responsibility was my refining fire.

I learned to discern danger before it entered a room.
I could feel the shift in the house before my mother ever said a word.
I knew how to pray peace into a tense atmosphere before I was taught the art of prayer.

God was teaching me the gift of spiritual sensitivity.
He was giving me the heart of a shepherd before I ever knew what that meant.
He was shaping a young intercessor who could feel things others missed—who could stand in the gap for people too weary to stand for themselves.

I thought I was surviving.
But I was being trained.

Not in a pulpit. Not in a classroom.
But in a broken home with two babies on my hips and the Holy Ghost on my side.

That was my first ministry.
And my first congregation was my family.

———

The Juggle Was Real — And So Was the Weight

To this day, I don't really know how I graduated from high school. Looking back, it feels like a blur—a delicate balancing act between exhaustion and sheer determination.

My grades were never terrible, but they were never a reflection of my true potential either. I wasn't a straight-A student, not because I lacked intelligence, but because I was too tired to focus and too burdened to breathe. My report cards were sprinkled with "Cs" and "Bs"—passing, yes—but barely holding up under the pressure I carried.

Some mornings, I'd make it to school just in time to turn in an assignment I had scribbled in between caring for Angel, running behind Bryan, and making sure Mama was stable enough to be left alone. Other days, I wouldn't make it to school at all.

There were days when my mother would call the school or simply show up at the front office with a desperate look in her eyes, asking them to send me home. And just like that, I was no longer a student—I was a caretaker again. A crisis manager. A stand-in mother. A reluctant rock holding everything together.

I remember sitting in the back of the classroom with my head down, not because I wasn't paying attention, but because I was calculating how many hours I had left before the house would fall apart again.

I'd watch other girls pass notes, plan weekend outings, talk about dances and crushes, and I'd sit silently—feeling like I lived in another world. Their biggest worry was who they were going to sit next to at lunch. Mine was whether Mama had eaten. Whether Angel had clean clothes. Whether Bryan was out of harm's way. Whether I'd be pulled out of class again because the walls were caving in on her… and nobody else was strong enough to hold them up.

———

Smart, But Buried Under Survival

It wasn't that I didn't have dreams.
I had plenty.

It wasn't that I couldn't learn.
I was hungry for knowledge.

But survival suffocated my focus.
My reality spoke louder than my assignments.
And the weight of trying to be the glue for a family that kept falling apart left little room for algebra and pre-calculus.

I would sit at the kitchen table after everyone else had fallen asleep and try to study, but my eyes would blur. My body would betray me with sleep before I could finish a chapter. And I'd pray—Lord, just help me get through this. Please, just don't let me fail.

And He did.

Somehow, someway, He carried me through.

I didn't walk across that graduation stage with cords or multiple scholarships, but I walked across it with honor. With a kind of triumph that no GPA could reflect. With a resilience that came from being pressed, but not crushed. From being overlooked, but not overtaken.

Because even when the system didn't see me…
Heaven did.

Even when teachers couldn't understand my struggle…

God was grading me on a higher scale.

I may not have been the valedictorian, but I was a warrior in a cap and gown.

———

I Walked the Stage Alone

I'll never forget the silence of that day.

My high school graduation was supposed to be a milestone—a celebration of perseverance, a crowning moment after years of sacrifice. It was the one day I had hoped would make all the struggle feel worth it. But it turned out to be the loneliest moment of my life.

No one came.

Not my mother.
Not my siblings.
Not a single aunt, uncle, or cousin.
No one.

As names were called and cheers erupted all around me, I sat quietly in my row, clutching the edges of my gown, holding back the swell of tears that threatened to drown me in front of hundreds of people. All around me, parents stood proudly with camcorders, balloons, flowers, and tear-stained smiles. Families gathered for photos and laughter. Some graduates leapt into the arms of loved ones.

I looked into the crowd for someone—anyone—familiar. But there was no one waving for me. No camera zooming in. No bouquet with my name on it. Just empty bleachers in the space where my people should have been.

It was supposed to be my moment.
But it became my mourning.

I walked across that stage alone, heard my name echo through the microphone: "Robin LaShea Welton," and received my diploma with a forced smile. Inside, my heart crumbled.
Because after all I had done… after all I had carried… there was no one there to witness the finish line.

———

The Giver Who Wanted to Be Held

That day exposed a deeper wound I had long tried to ignore:
I wanted to belong.
I craved family—not the kind I had to keep rescuing, but the kind that could see me, nurture me, and pour back into me.

I wanted arms to wrap around me and say, *"You did it. I'm proud of you."*

I wanted someone to fix my hair that morning and tell me how beautiful I looked in my cap and gown.

I wanted a hand to hold mine, not because I was carrying them—but because they were carrying me.

I was so tired of being the strong one. The responsible one. The stand-in mama. The crisis manager. The emotional lifeguard.
I didn't want to be the giver that day.

I wanted to be gathered.

I wanted to be the child for once… not the one holding everyone together while silently falling apart.

But that wasn't my story—at least not then.

God was writing something different. Something deeper.

He was planting a hunger in me—not just for earthly family, but for divine belonging. He was stirring a craving in me that no earthly arms could satisfy, a longing to be nurtured by something eternal. Something holy. Something that would never walk away or forget me.

Chapter 3

Crossroads. A new voice, a new place.

Drawn to the fire, unaware of the flame.

I was walking with God, consecrated and committed, carving out a life of obedience in the midst of my youth. I was the girl who said no to compromise, who fasted while others flirted with rebellion. I was the one who stayed in church or home while others went to dances and parties. My heart was tethered to God's will, but my humanity still craved connection. I was lonely, not for God. He was near, but for people, for friendship, for the warmth of shared laughter and conversation. Because the truth is, when you're young and so like God, the crowd gets smaller, the circle gets quieter, and sometimes consecration feels like isolation. That's when He appeared, the one I wouldn't have given the time of day to before.

But hunger changes your appetite, and because I was hungry for interaction, I mistook familiarity for safety and charisma for character. He was what I call a professional Christian. I will use a fictional name as to not expose him. Clarence spoke the language, had the rhythm of religion, and knew just enough words to be impressive. And so, I opened up. He saw my hunger and gave me attention. He invited me to church, and I said yes. What started as spiritual companionship turned quickly into something else. Lines blurred, boundaries crossed. The anointing I admired couldn't cover the compromise I allowed. And though I felt terrible, I kept repenting and remained in a relationship with him, because by then, I had done what many of us do. I gave Him a role God never assigned, and I told myself this was my husband, that God had authored this connection. I addressed my need in spiritual language, and I called it destiny. I thought that Clarence was my husband because it was just not many saved young men to pick from.

Then one evening after choir rehearsal, we drove past the house of his spiritual father. He waved. The man of God whistled for him to come back. We turned around. It was the moment my spirit had unknowingly been waiting for. There on that porch, I met Apostle S.E. McKinney, the man I had heard so much about from Clarence. His name had already become a legend in my ears, but it was his voice that would crack something open in me. He greeted us and then took us into the house. We sat down, and without warning, he began to teach. But this wasn't teaching. It was revelation. This was as if he pulled the veil back on Scripture and walked us into the living Word. He preached like he had walked with Jesus that morning. He taught as if he had dined with the patriarchs and conversed with the prophets. He didn't just quote the Word. He unveiled it, and I was undone. This was no ordinary man, and this was no ordinary moment. God had just introduced me to a new voice and a new place. When we got up to leave, he called the young man back. Wait, he said, I need to speak with you. I waited in the car, unaware that upstairs in the prayer room, a prophetic conversation was taking place. A divine recognition was being spoken. The apostle said, this one is different. She's not like others you've brought. The hand of God is on her life. She's marked. She belongs to God. And if you mishandle her, God will deal with you. That was the beginning of my next becoming. I didn't know it yet, but that moment was the collision of purpose and transition. God was calling me out of what I had been suffering for into what he had truly assigned me. The fire I was drawn to wasn't just the fire of charisma. It was the fire of refinement. And this man, would ignite both pain and purpose. He would stir my gift and silence my discernment. He would mark me for better and for worse. But in that moment, all I knew was this. I had come to a crossroad and the fire had found me.

The first time I heard him preach, I was hooked, like a person addicted to a drug they never expected to need. First preacher I ever could listen to for 4 hours without getting bored. It wasn't just a message. It was an encounter. A collision of glory and revelation that ignited something in me. I didn't know I was dry. I had grown up in the church. I heard great preaching. But this, this was different. The way he unveiled the word, it was like he could see through the pages into the very mind of God. It wasn't just teaching. It was revelation. And I wanted more. Every time I heard he was preaching, I rearranged my world to be there. I couldn't get enough. And every service was otherworldly. The weight of glory that fell in the room left us trembling and transformed. People were being healed. Yokes were breaking. The altars were wet with tears and saturated with oil. That young man and I, along with a few other young people, joined his ministry without hesitation. We weren't just attendees. We were becoming disciples. We learned how to pray with authority, how to preach with precision, and how to walk in a level of prophetic revelation that most people would have dreamed of. We were in awe of what God was doing in us. But one day everything began to unravel.

Because the church was evangelistic in nature, we traveled a great deal, I traveled with them often and would sometimes stay with them. This particular time I'd just bathed and stepped into the bedroom after spending the night with the McKinney's, sleeping with his wife while he stayed upstairs in the prayer room. I went back in there to get dressed. I was putting on my bra when the man of God opened the door without knocking. He saw me. I froze. He quickly closed the door. Months later he told me I couldn't get that image out of my head. That moment, was the beginning of something unraveling that I didn't see coming.

This is where I chose to be transparent; not to expose shame, but to expose the kind of manipulation that masquerades as mentorship. That day was not just a physical moment. It was a spiritual violation. I was uncovered. Not just my body, but left without proper protection.

In the spirit, where was his wife? That question has echoed through my soul for years. Not out of blame, but out of forgiveness. I don't know where she was and how she never came back into the room.

However, I know that spiritual houses, just like natural ones, are built on order. And that order had already been breached before he ever opened the door. Whether it was intentional or a moment of carelessness, the truth is there were no safeguards in place. And when there is no order, the enemy exploits the chaos. 1 Thessalonians 5:22 in the King James Version it says: "Abstain from all appearance of evil." The issue is not just what happened, but what was allowed to happen. Being in that house, in that room, alone and unclothed violated the appearance of holiness. Even if there had been no immediate touch or action, cause it wasn't —at least not that time.

The Holy Spirit commands those in spiritual leadership to operate above reproach. Not just for the sake of others, but because of the high stakes of their influence. 1 Timothy 3:2 - New International Version "The overseer is to be above reproach, faithful to his wife, temperate, self-controlled, respectful, hospitable, able to teach." Where was the faithfulness to his wife, to his assignment, to the vulnerable sheep in his care?

This moment marked the crack in the structure, one that let the enemy slither in.

Genesis 3:7 reminds us that the moment Adam and Eve ate the fruit, they realized they were naked and uncovered and they hid. And in that room, what should have been covered by marital boundaries, pastoral accountability, and spiritual protection was instead exposed and unguarded.

The Setup — When Naivety Meets Neglect

I was just seventeen. A girl with fire in her soul and purity in her intentions. I wasn't dressing for attention. I wasn't luring anyone. I was simply hungry for God. Pure. Passionate. Naive. But the enemy doesn't just prey on impurity — he preys on opportunity. And sometimes, the setup is crafted not from sin, but from sorrow, vulnerability, and open wounds.

He was a man of God. Married. Anointed. A target for the enemy. Here I am a young lady, uncovered and naive. I fully respected him and was afraid to do anything wrong in the presence of the McKinney's. I now know I was at the wrong place. No young single young lady should be staying with a married couple. That's a mess waiting to happen. I was never taught that. I was just so eager to be around this powerful couple. I was a silly young lady fascinated by the anointing. Satan saw this and worked his mojo.

Just like David, who should've been on the battlefield but instead stayed behind to watch Bathsheba bathe, this leader was out of position. And when spiritual leaders abandon their post, they don't fall alone — they take others with them.

Covering Matters

In Scripture, covering is about protection. Boaz covered Ruth with his garment as a sign of covenant and safety (Ruth 3:9). Priests were given sacred instructions in Leviticus 16 to protect people from unauthorized exposure to holy things. Why? Because boundaries preserve life — spiritually, emotionally, and physically.

But that day, boundaries weren't just blurred — they were obliterated.

When someone walks in on you undressed — emotionally, spiritually, or physically — they should walk out and reestablish the boundary. He didn't. He crossed a threshold not just of a room, but of trust, of order, of sacred space. I should never have been uncovered in that way — not by him, not in that place, not under the name of mentorship or ministry.

He should have turned away immediately.
He should have knocked.
He should have guarded the gate.
Instead, he fed a fantasy. I found out many months later that he was walking by and the door was slightly cracked and he saw my breast and opened the door.

And if this was Satan setting a trap, he didn't avoid it — he partnered with it, because what happened next was premeditated manipulation.

———

DC: Where the Walls Fell

A few days later, we were invited to Washington, D.C. for ministry. It was there he began weaving a more calculated plan.

Days before he told me I needed to get his godson "out of my spirit." Then, in front of me, he asked Clarence if he loved me. "Not like that," the young man replied coldly.

My soul shattered. I had been praying and fasting inquiring God if he was my husband.

I cried for days — over the dream I had attached to him. I thought we were building something sacred; instead, I was just another young lady with misplaced hope.

But that rejection, I see now was a set up. He knew that young man wasn't into me like that and he knew being embarrassed like that would devastate me.

That was a power move to clear the emotional path — to break me down and then he could rebuild me in his image. What I thought was pastoral care was strategic control. Session after session, he "counseled" me through heartbreak — dissecting my soul, digging into private wounds, telling me who I was and why I was broken. And then he presented himself as the healer, the answer, the only voice I needed.

The Conditioning

One day in D.C., I asked permission to visit family for a few hours. He agreed. No curfew. No rules. I returned as promised. But when I walked back in, everything changed.

He rebuked me harshly, accusing me of rebellion and disrespect. He declared I was insubordinate and said I needed to be sent home — like a child being punished for breaking an unspoken rule.

The next day, he told his wife, "I'm taking her back to her mother."

No escort. No accountability. Just him and me in a car, headed to North Carolina.

During the ride, he brought it up again — the rejection, the young man, the shame. We dissected my pain again, but this time it wasn't under the guise of healing. This time, it was isolation.

He didn't take me to my mother's house.

He took me to his.

He hugged me. Told me he only wanted the best for me.

Then he kissed me.

Then he touched me.

I froze.

Seventeen. Confused. Vulnerable. Honored to have his attention. Afraid to reject the man who had taught me how to hear God. I didn't have the language for it then, but now I know — that wasn't mentorship. It was manipulation. That wasn't fathering. That was grooming.

The Burned Man

Before the bishop, the prophet, the revelator — he was a broken boy.

I had heard him tell the story many times… At five years old, he had been burned in a house. The scars on his body were deep. His neck was disfigured. His skin permanently altered. He carried those wounds into adulthood and then into ministry.

He told stories of being bullied — called "burned meat," teased and laughed at. He was never the one girls chased. He learned early that he had to lead to be seen, that his value wasn't in beauty but in power. And somehow, that pain became a tool. A license. A permission slip to do whatever it took to feel wanted.

I saw his scars. I understood his sorrow. And that's what made it all more confusing. I didn't want to hurt him. I didn't want to wound him again. So I stayed silent — thinking silence was compassion.

If I had of known that me not rebuking him and telling what he did would imprison me for almost a lifetime, I would have ran for my life! I would have ran home to my mother. I would have got in touch with my biological father and moved to Atlanta Georgia. This was the worst mistake of my life. I didn't have the emotional intelligence to know how to respond or to think my way out of this trap. So young ladies, you don't have to show pity when someone is out of line with you. I don't care who they are, don't you let them violate you. Tell it! The truth will always prevail! Don't remain silent like I did. I could have saved myself decades of suffering.

———

The Second Violation

Nothing more happened that day. Just a kiss. A touch. A confusing silence. But it was enough to rewrite how I saw myself.

To my surprise, he drove me back to D.C. The air was different. Thick with unspoken tension. His wife, the other women in ministry, even his sons — they looked at me with suspicion. Judgment. Distance.

I had become the silent scandal.

The First Lady and I never recovered. Her stares were icy. Her presence sharp. And in the middle of it all, I kept wondering: *Why didn't you cover me?* Why didn't you come with him? But I dared not say a word. She was protecting her marriage after the fact. I was trying to salvage what was left of my dignity.

And I had been here before.

———

The Pattern Repeats

Years earlier, I was staying with my cousin and her military husband. One morning, I was asleep, he walked into my room in nothing but a towel. Sat on my bed. Rubbed my back. I froze — pretended to be still asleep. It happened again the next morning.

This time I spoke up.

And I was sent home. Labeled a liar. Treated like the problem.

So here I was again.

Another adult man. Another moment of courage swallowed by fear. And Satan whispered: *Don't say anything. They didn't believe you last time. They won't believe you now.*

And tragically, I listened.

That silence became a chain. A muzzle forged in fear and fastened by shame.

———

The Voice That Was Muzzled

Death and life are in the power of the tongue (Proverbs 18:21).

But when I chose silence, I forfeited my voice. And when your voice goes silent, your spirit begins to die.

The enemy didn't just want my body. He wanted my boldness.
He didn't just want to tamper with my purity — he wanted to assassinate my purpose.
He wanted me to believe I was the villain in every room, the one who always gets it wrong, the repeat offense.

And the evidence stacked up:
- My biological father abandoned me.
- My mother sent me away to pursue her dreams.
- I was raped by an older boy in the neighborhood.
- My cousin's husband touched me inappropriately.
- Now the man of God — the one I revered — crossed the line.

So I buried it all. Buried the story. Buried the truth.

Not realizing, I was also burying my strength.

―――

Fear in Disguise

"For God has not given us the spirit of fear, but of power, love, and a sound mind."
— 2 Timothy 1:7

But fear came anyway. And it dressed up like wisdom. It told me silence was strength. That meekness meant secrecy. That loyalty meant invisibility.

It wasn't true.

My silence didn't save his ministry. That man had a global message, an apostolic mantle but God would not bless his ministry the way he should have because of this secret unconfessed sin.

It didn't preserve peace.
It only broke me.

What if I had spoken up?
What if I had the voice, the vocabulary, the audacity to draw a line when the first one was crossed? What if I had been equipped—not

just with Scripture, but with sense, not just with hunger for God, but with the wisdom to discern wolves from shepherds?

Maybe the years of bondage could have been broken before they ever began.

Maybe the manipulation wouldn't have metastasized into a full-blown system, complete with altars, armor bearers, and applause.

Maybe I wouldn't have lost my mother—to distance that turned into death. Maybe my siblings and I would still have memories un-cluttered by trauma, unshattered by silence.

Because that's what my silence became—a prison with no locks, only assumptions.

People mistook my quiet for compliance.

They thought I agreed because I didn't scream.

They thought I was loyal because I stayed.

But I wasn't loyal.

I was lost.

And the worst part? Others followed my silence.

They trusted my trust. They echoed my example.

I didn't know that my hesitation to speak would be interpreted as validation.

I didn't realize that the way I staggered under the weight of confu-sion looked like devotion to those watching from afar.

They couldn't see the internal hemorrhaging.

They just saw me *still there*, still smiling, still lifting hands.

And they thought, *"If she's still standing, it must be safe."*

But it wasn't safe.

It was spiritual sabotage in slow motion.

And we were all caught in it.

The thing about deception is—it doesn't always come dressed in darkness.

Sometimes it wears white robes, designer suits and holds a microphone.

Sometimes it sounds like prophecy but moves like control.

Sometimes it calls itself "covering" while quietly cutting off your access to every other voice that loves you.

Wisdom is the principal thing. Therefore get wisdom: and with all thy getting, get understanding. (Proverbs 4:7)

I wish I had that wisdom then.

But wisdom rarely walks with you at the start.

It waits in the wreckage.

It grows in the ashes.

It's forged in the furnace of hindsight, cultivated in the soil of sorrow.

And yet—even there—God is not wasteful.

He doesn't discard pain.

He doesn't ignore the years we lost or the tears we never got to cry in real time.

Somehow, even what I failed to say then has become the very thing I declare now.

What I couldn't name in my youth, I now speak with sacred clarity.

What I didn't confront back then, I now uncover.

What I once survived in silence, I now dismantle with truth.

Because silence is no longer my survival tactic—truth is.

When we got back from that revival, my world didn't just shift—it shattered.

My mother, my final line of natural defense, had packed my clothes into bags and placed them on the porch. Neatly. Deliberately.

On the door was a letter:

"If you're going to keep following that ministry, you can't stay here."

That moment didn't just break me.

It split me.

Emotionally, spiritually, structurally.

Everything I had known as home was severed with one decision.

But I didn't see her warning as love.

I saw it as warfare.

I thought she was being used by the enemy to stop my 'elevation.'

Because that's what I'd been taught: anyone who questions the leader is being used by the devil.

So I picked up my bags—and walked away from the last place that truly loved me.

"The simple believe every word: but the prudent consider well their steps." (Proverbs 14:15)

But I wasn't prudent. I was programmed.

I didn't know discernment—I only knew doctrine.

I couldn't distinguish control from calling.

I had no language for abuse when it came wrapped in Scripture and shouted with tongues.

My identity was still fragile, my mind still forming. I thought because the man of God was so accurate in the prophetic that questioning him would be a sin.

And the dissonance was too much:

How could someone so anointed also be so abusive?

How could someone who healed the sick leave so many emotionally bleeding in his wake?

How could someone who spoke in tongues be weaponizing them behind closed doors?

Here's the part they don't teach you in church:

God can use people He hasn't approved.

The anointing may be authentic, but the character behind it may be corrupted.

Yes, the glory was real. Yes, the miracles happened.

But gifting is not godliness.

Revelation is not righteousness.

The gifts and callings of God are without repentance. (Romans 11:29)

Which means someone can be used by God while simultaneously being manipulated by darkness.

It took me decades to understand that duality.

Decades to stop blaming myself for being duped.

Decades to unravel the guilt of not walking away sooner.

But now I know—it wasn't weakness.

It was unfinishedness.

I wasn't rebellious—I was misled.

I didn't betray my mother—I was torn from her, led away by someone who called it "destiny" while dismantling my identity.

And now?

Now I speak—not just for myself, but for every daughter who didn't have the words, the wisdom, or the will to say, *"This is not God."*

I speak for those who still carry wounds in their worship.

I speak for the ones who shouted "Hallelujah" while silently hemorrhaging.

I speak for the ones who were never taught that real authority never isolates—it protects.

That real covering doesn't confiscate—it empowers.

That real leadership doesn't demand loyalty at the cost of your soul or your body.

I was once silenced by fear.

Now, I'm fueled by truth.

And I will not be quiet again.

A Letter to the Girl I Was

From the Woman I Survived to Become

Hey, Baby girl.

I see you—standing there on that porch, clutching a letter in one hand and your identity in the other. Your life is stuffed into garbage bags, but your faith is still intact. I see the storm behind your eyes, the silent war in your mind, the tears you've tucked away because strength, they told you, meant silence.
You thought this was the price of the anointing.
You thought leaving your mother meant proving your loyalty to God.
You thought being torn apart was part of being set apart.
But let me whisper something sacred into your soul:
You were never meant to pay for ministry with your personhood.

You were never called to trade your safety for spiritual performance.
You were never supposed to be confused between deliverance and domination, between leadership and control.
And no matter how powerful he sounded, your discernment wasn't broken—it was buried, beneath layers of manipulation, beneath twisted theology and weaponized Scripture.

You didn't fail.
You were *forged*.
Forged in a fire you never asked for.

Shaped in the shadows of a system that confused charisma for character.

You walked through a wilderness that was never yours to inherit, and yet—God never lost track of you. Not for one moment.

I know you felt abandoned.
I know you wrestled with the lie that you had to choose between covenant and calling.
But hear me now with clarity: God never required your isolation.
God never demanded that you walk away from family to follow Him.
That wasn't holiness. That was control.
That wasn't consecration. That was grooming.
It wasn't God who stripped you. It was man who exploited what you didn't yet understand.

So let me say what no one said to you then.
Let me be the voice you needed in the silence:

I'm sorry.

I'm sorry he used the pulpit to cloak perversion.
I'm sorry he weaponized the Word against your womanhood.
I'm sorry your innocence became the battleground of his brokenness.
I'm sorry the sacred was twisted into something suffocating.
But hear me:

You were never the problem. You were the prize.
You are not the mistake.
You are the miracle.
You are not the villain in this story.
You are the vessel God Himself has redeemed—cleansed, healed, and called again.

So hold your head high, baby girl.
You didn't abandon love—you survived a system that paraded abuse in garments of glory.
You didn't fall from grace—you walked through fire and didn't burn.
And now?

Now you're not just healing. You're heralding.
You're sounding the alarm for every daughter still stuck in silence.
You're pulling others out of pits you once called home.
You're rebuilding altars, not just for worship—but for *truth*.
You are no longer buried beneath the weight of what happened.
You are being rebuilt upon the foundation of who you are:
Chosen.
Cherished.
Called.
Whole.

And if no one ever told you:
You were worth saving all along.

You are the woman I fought to become.

You are the echo of every prayer I prayed in the dark.

You are not broken.

You are becoming.

With fierce love,

Me—

The woman you survived to become.

A Prayer for the Trapped, the Torn, and the Tired

Father, in the matchless name of Jesus—

We come on behalf of every daughter who is silently suffocating under the weight of spiritual deception.

For every heart that is bleeding behind the veil of "faithfulness," for every soul that is stuck in the space between *revelation and violation,*

we cry out to the God who sees—El Roi—the God who *never misses a moment.*

You see what others overlook.

You see behind the pulpits and beyond the platforms.

You see through the prophetic words that are laced with performance and control.

You see past the charisma into the cracks of compromised character.

You see behind the honor culture that silences questions and canonizes abusers.

You are not blinded by religious performance.
You are not deaf to the cries muffled by fear, nor are You distant from the rooms religion tried to lock You out of.
You walk into the back rooms of church hurt.
You sit beside the daughters who cry on sanctuary floors after the benediction.
You hover over the hearts that don't know if they're discerning or just damaged.

So now, Abba,
Stretch out your hand and break every spiritual chain.
Disentangle every heart that has been tied to control in the name of covering.
Sever every soul tie dressed up as mentorship.
Disarm every manipulative voice that twisted Scripture into shackles.
Resurrect discernment, Lord.
Let it come alive again—sharp, clear, holy, and unapologetic.

Heal what religion wounded.
Rebuild what false loyalty broke.
Cover every daughter whose identity was shattered in the name of submission.

Guard their minds from shame and their hearts from internalizing what was never their fault.

Deliver them from the need to be chosen by someone who was never submitted to You.

Give them an exit strategy that doesn't cost their soul.

Raise up safe houses and people —true intercessors, not spectators.

Send them friends who protect, not just applaud.

Let every woman know she is *not alone*.

Let her know that freedom is not rebellion and that leaving toxicity is not leaving You.

Let her know that You still want her, still see her, still have a purpose for her.

Let the captives come out with clarity, not confusion.

With boldness, not bitterness.

With wisdom, not wounds.

And for the ones still stuck—God, be the voice in their silence.

Be the strength in their no.

Be the fire in their escape.

Let them find their way out—without losing themselves.

In the mighty name of Jesus,
Amen.

———

A Declaration for the Daughters in the Dark

To every woman bound in silence:
I declare that your voice is rising.
Your story matters. Your pain is valid. Your process is sacred.
You are not crazy. You are not dramatic. You are not imagining things.
What happened to you was real—and *so is your healing.*

No more confusing bondage with loyalty.
No more protecting dysfunction just to remain accepted.
No more shrinking to fit someone else's idea of submission.
No more allowing guilt to dress up as honor.

You are breaking free from systems that used your sincerity as a leash.
You are divorcing the doctrine that taught you to suffer in silence.
You are walking away—not from your calling, but from what tried to counterfeit it.

The God who called you is the same God who is rescuing you.
And He is not late.
You are coming out—*with your mind intact, your heart still tender, and your spirit stronger than ever.*
You are coming out with your dignity restored and your identity reawakened.

You are coming out as one who will no longer hide in the pews of performance but will stand in the pulpit of purpose.

You are not the only one this happened to—
But you will be one of the last it happens to on your watch.

Your healing is a weapon.
Your testimony is a key.
Your life is a lighthouse—and daughters lost in the storm will find home through your light.

You are not overlooked.
You are not discarded.
You are not disqualified.
You are loved. You are chosen. You are free.

In Jesus' name,
Amen.

Chapter 4

A Servant in the House

My first stop after my mother put me out was the modest home of a kind-hearted woman named Sister Essie. She's gone now—transitioned from this life—but I carry her memory like a bookmark in the early chapters of my journey. She lived in the E.B. Jordan Community Apartments, just a short walk from where our fledgling ministry held services in the neighborhood center. It all seemed divinely orchestrated. Church was right around the corner, the Spirit of God was moving, and for the first time, my calling was beginning to come into focus.

I was invited to preach my initial sermon, and the ministry celebrated it. Everyone rejoiced—everyone, except Sister Essie. That's when something shifted. Jealousy crept in, subtle at first, but soon it consumed her. She couldn't understand why God would choose someone as young and inexperienced as me to preach the gospel—and not her. What started as quiet resentment soon turned to outright rejection. One day, without warning or explanation, she asked me to leave. Just like that. Another door closed. Another person turned me away.

And the message that began echoing in my spirit was painfully clear:

You don't belong unless you bend. You won't be kept unless you conform.

Without realizing it, I was being conditioned.
Don't cause friction.
Don't stand out.
Just serve.
Just survive.

You have to understand—I had nowhere to go. I was young, broke, and abandoned and told going to college as not God's choice for me.
My mother had closed the door behind me, and the rest of my family wasn't an option. That's when Apostle McKinney called a family meeting. He stood in the living room and told everyone I had no place to stay. The decision was unanimous: I would move in with them.

At first, it felt like the family I never had. His sons— my brothers— welcomed me with warmth. Robert, the eldest, even gave up his room so I'd have a space of my own. For a brief moment, I felt safe.

But safety soon became servitude.

Not because they asked me to. But because the house was filthy— neglected, bug-infested, and cluttered. I had come from a middle-class home. We were homeowners. My understanding of order and care looked nothing like what I saw in that house. So I did what needed to be done. I started scrubbing, cleaning, organizing. I cooked three meals a day. I served both Apostle and Lady McKinney breakfast in bed. I mopped every floor. I did everything—not out of joy, not even out of duty—but out of desperation. I needed to earn my keep. I needed to be useful, invisible, small.

Somewhere along the way, I stopped being a guest and became a maid. A housekeeper. A servant. And still, I asked if I could get a job—just something small, to earn income, build savings, maybe find a way forward. The answer was a resounding no.

"God wants you in full-time ministry," I was told.
"Just like us."

But looking back now, I see it for what it really was: control.

A job would have meant options. A job meant independence.
A job meant freedom. And he couldn't risk me getting free.
So he cloaked control in religious language:
Staying broke is submission.
Dependence is obedience.
Isolation is consecration.

And the chains got tighter.

At some point, the line between calling and captivity blurred. I had no income, no access to resources, no family to turn to, no home of my own. I depended on Apostle McKinney for everything. And that is a *dangerous* place for any young woman to be. Always remember this: "Never let a man give you anything because it's not for free!"

Then the advances began.
First subtle, then stronger.
What began as spiritual mentorship became emotional manipulation, and eventually, physical violation.

These weren't consensual moments.
They were compliance-driven.
When you're surviving, silence feels safer than speaking.
And fear can wear the mask of loyalty when you're just trying to avoid homelessness.

I felt dirty.
Ashamed.
Violated.
But I said nothing.

Because saying something meant losing the only roof over my head.
And this wasn't gossip-level humiliation.
This was soul-level grief.

The kind of grief that comes when someone touches you whom you don't desire.

When someone kisses you and your insides turn—not with butterflies, but with dread.

And still, you stay still.

Not because you want to—but because you're trying to survive another night.

Just writing this brings it all back.

Every week was a countdown.

Would he come in my room again?

Would he touch me again?

By now, he wasn't even sleeping with his wife.

And I had become his stand-in. His secret. His scapegoat.

I hated every second of it.

I tried to run—countless times.

But each time I did, he'd track me down—not just physically, but spiritually.

He'd flip the narrative.

Gather the saints.

Preach over the pulpit:

"She's running from her call."

And they believed him.

No one ever questioned the apostle.

I was a prisoner—trapped in a house called ministry.

By then, my mother had remarried and moved to New York.

Both my grandparents were gone.

And I had no connection with my biological father's side of the family.

I reached out to my stepfather once for financial help with the small business I'd tried to start—but he declined. I couldn't ask him for shelter. He wasn't my blood, and he didn't owe me that.

So where could I go?

When even the sanctuary becomes a snare—where do you run?

So I stayed.

Stayed in the cycle.

Stayed in the silence.

Stayed until I was numb.

I begged God for deliverance.

I cried on cold, bare floors.

I worshiped while bleeding internally.

And heaven felt silent—like God had chosen sides, and it wasn't mine.

How could he still preach?

How could he raise his voice in glory while mine was gagged in grief? So I had this brilliant idea, if God's idea of changing Abraham's name was prophetic in that every time he heard his name, he believed that God would make him a father; I need to become a full fledged McKinney. No one from my family came to rescue me. If I change my name and allowed them to adopt me then maybe he would change! Realize that I'm his daughter and rectify what he has done. I will never forget his first reaction- he didn't want me to do that, but I wanted the man of God to become accountable and honorable. I had forgiven him but if I had to stay and couldn't get the finances to get my own place. I was going to do it right. We went to file adoption papers but because I was 18, the judge told me I could legally change my name for less than the grueling process of adoption. I pawned my class ring and paid for my legal name change from Robin LaShea Welton to LaShea Victoria McKinney. I never liked my first name anyway. I was always picked on in school by people asking me where was Batman? The first time First Lady heard my middle name LaShea she never called me Robin again. Then one night we went to a revival and a white evangelist named Evangelist Gatlin called me up and said: God has changed your name and when God changes your name, he changes your destiny. Our church went up in praise because First Lady had been calling me LaShea which was my mother's middle name too by the way. Victoria was a name that apostle named me. He said I had the class of a Victoria. McKinney was the family I had now become a part of. But, that name change didn't refocus him. He would not leave me alone.

When a leader is genuinely anointed but refuses to remain submitted to God, the anointing becomes a weapon.
The enemy doesn't always counterfeit—sometimes he corrupts the real thing.

He pollutes pure callings with entitlement, lust, and secrecy.
And when that leader stops surrendering daily, they start *using* people instead of *serving* them.

You're no longer their assignment.
You're their pawn.

The tragedy isn't that they were once gifted.
The tragedy is that they stopped being governed.

They preach holiness in public, but stop pursuing it in private.
They cast out devils but refuse to cast down their own imaginations.
They lay hands on others while refusing to lift their own in surrender.

And now?
They're gifted, charismatic, and fallen.
Wounded themselves—and now wounding others.
What started in power became polluted by sin.

The ones they were sent to *cover*, they uncovered.

But this isn't the end.

"Be sure your sin will find you out." — Numbers 32:23

You didn't get away with anything.
God saw it all.
But exposure is not punishment.
It's *mercy*.

It's a divine interruption before your soul collapses completely.

"But I discipline my body and keep it under control, lest after preaching to others I myself should be disqualified." — 1 Corinthians 9:27

Paul reminds us: gifts don't guarantee godliness.
You can win souls and still lose your own if you refuse to crucify the flesh daily.

David knew this feeling.
A man after God's own heart who took what wasn't his.

But when he finally repented, God didn't just *restore* him—He *refined* him.

"Create in me a clean heart, O God, and renew a right spirit within me." — Psalm 51:10

This is your Psalm 51 moment.

The Bible says:

> "Restore to me the joy of your salvation, and uphold me with a willing spirit. Then I will teach transgressors your ways, and sinners will return to you." (Psalm 51:12–13)

> You were never meant to stay fallen.
> You were meant to return—to repentance, to righteousness, to reverence.
> Let the refining begin.

Your recovery can lead to someone else's rescue. But let's be clear — it *starts* with repentance.
Not charm.
Not crocodile tears.
Not another conference or a cleverly crafted sermon.
Real repentance.

To the fallen pastor reading this — hear me:
You're *not* beyond redemption.
But make no mistake: you are dangerously out of alignment.

God is not impressed with your platform.

He's after your posture.

He wants your heart, not your hype.

Not the crowd you've gathered. Not the pulpit you've polished. Not the fake humility you wear like cologne.

Yes — you did damage.

Yes — you misused your influence.

Yes — you wounded people God trusted you to cover.

But if you *truly* turn — not just in public, but in private — your story can still serve a purpose.

Your fall can become someone else's warning sign.

Your mess can become a map — if you'll stop hiding behind your gift and finally face your guilt.

Don't let your legacy be the tale of an anointing that turned abusive.

Don't let your name become a cautionary tale whispered behind closed doors.

Let it be known that you came back to the altar — not polished, but repentant.

Not powerful, but pierced.

Not respected, but real.

And to the ones who know this pain — the daughters, the sons, the servants in the house who were violated in the name of "spiritual covering" — I see you. I *am* you.

I cried out to God, night after night. But the heavens stayed quiet.

No thunder.

No lightning.

Just the sound of the same voice that defiled me at night… preaching with power in the pulpit by morning.

It was maddening.

It was spiritual vertigo.

How could God *use* a man like that?

I whispered it into my pillow, while his room sat right across the hall.

I wondered, *How can he speak with such revelation, yet live with such rot?*

I didn't understand it then — that gifting can flow even when character is in full decay.

That a man like Saul could still prophesy on the road to his own destruction.

(1 Samuel 19:24 — go read it for yourself.)

I saw myself in *The Color Purple*.

In Celie — lying still, lifeless, numb.

Used, not loved.

Obligated, not cherished.

Serving in the kitchen and the bedroom.

He wasn't making love — he was taking something.

And when it was over, she was just… there. Staring at the ceiling. Waiting for it to end.

That was me.

Then I watched *A Jazzman's Blues*.
That young girl, bent over by her own grandfather — not out of desire, but survival.
Payment for a place to stay.
That scene shattered me. Because it wasn't just a movie — it was my memory.

And then there was Joyce Meyer — sharing her testimony about her own father.
Her own flesh and blood molesting her for years.
And yet she forgave him.
When I heard her story, something broke open in me.

I realized I wasn't the only one.
And tragically, I won't be the last.

But maybe — just maybe — if I tell the *whole* truth,
If I stop hiding behind church language and prophetic titles,
If I expose what religion tried to suppress,
Then maybe some daughter can find the strength to leave.
Maybe she won't stay silent like I did.
Maybe she won't waste 36 years trying to be good enough to be safe.

Let me be clear:

You do not have to earn your right to exist.
You do not have to perform to deserve protection.
You do not have to be silent to be spiritual.

And to the leaders who have fallen:
This is your *window*.
This is your *mercy moment*.
Don't waste it trying to maintain your image.

Repent.
Return.
And rebuild.
Not your brand — your soul.

Because if God can heal me — and He did— then He can redeem you.
But only if you come clean.

A Prophetic Charge to the Church: Stop Protecting What God Wants to Purge

To the Body of Christ: Enough is enough!
You have mourned your platforms more than your people.
You have protected personalities while burying victims.

You have anointed abusers and silenced survivors — in the name of order, in the name of loyalty, in the name of "God's anointed."

But let me say this clearly:
God is not pleased.
And He is pulling the cover off every compromise.

This is your warning.
This is your wake-up call.
You cannot rebuke Jezebel while enabling Eli.
In other words, you can't claim to confront or expose the spirit of Jezebel (manipulation, control, seduction, rebellion) if you're at the same time protecting or excusing the spirit of Eli (a system which tolerates sin, refuses to confront wrong, and enables corruption by being passive). If you're going to call out Jezebel but allow Eli to keep enabling her, you're undermining your own stand. The Jezebel spirit thrives because Eli's spirit gives it room to operate.

You have built ministries on charisma and not character.
You have ignored discernment in favor of influence.
You have called it "spiritual fathering" when it was grooming.
You've labeled it "mentorship" while it was manipulation.

Where were the watchmen?
Where were the intercessors when the sheep were bleeding?

Why did you praise his preaching while women sat in pews, broken and numb, pretending to be whole? I've always wanted to ask this but never had the courage
till now. I'm sure after reading my book, lots of you will say I always knew something wasn't right! If that's you, shame on you! My blood is on your hands too. You didn't ask God to help you, help me. Did you pray for me? Did you sit the man of God down and tell him what God was revealing to you? No, because you thought this was consensual. Still, where was the council of leadership that makes men of God accountable? Where were the Global council of mothers that checked in on the women in ministry, a safe place for them to seek help, a refuge to run without you gossiping and telling their business?

Instead you all kept calling him back to your church because the man had a message. His prophecies came to pass. He was skillful, had much wisdom, just not enough to fix his own life. Imagine what that man could have been if he had been accountable. The Kingdom needed that anointing but there were no safeguards in place to salvage, protect, and redirect him.

Church, we've got to do something about that moving forward!

Woe to the Church that coddles gifted wolves and crucifies bleeding lambs.

The altar is not a stage.
The pulpit is not a performance platform.

And the anointing is not a pass for perversion.

You keep shouting about revival — but God says, *first comes repentance.*
You want fire, but you refuse the refining.
You want harvest, but you ignore the hidden rot in your foundation.

This is not just a scandal.
It's a system.
And God is calling His Church to dismantle the altars built in man's name and return to holiness.

Here's the charge:

- ❖ Stop silencing the voices of the violated to preserve the reputation of the revered.
- ❖ Stop calling victims bitter when all they did was tell the truth.
- ❖ Stop labeling whistleblowers rebellious when they're just revealing what God exposed.
- ❖ Stop treating giftedness like godliness. They are not the same.
- ❖ Stop platforming people who have never passed the test of private integrity.

The Church must repent.

Not just individually, but *institutionally*.

You must cleanse the altar.

You must confront your favorites.

You must tear down idols in collars and robes.

Because God is tired of sharing His glory with men who molest His sheep!

If the Church won't purify herself, God will purify her by force. And when He does, it won't be quiet. It won't be clean. It will be public. It will be painful. But it will be holy.

This is a divine interruption.

This is exposure as mercy.

This is judgment that begins in the house of God.

So rise, Church.

With tears. With trembling. With truth.

Be the house where healing can happen.

Be the house where repentance is real.

Be the house where the abused don't have to sit next to their abuser to prove they're spiritual.

Be the house where holiness returns to the center.

Because God is raising up a pure remnant — a people who value His presence over platforms, truth over titles, healing over hiding.

Clean house.

Return to the altar.

And let the fear of the Lord fall again.

Chapter 5

The Child I Never Got to Hold —
And the Years I'll Never Get Back

It was a summer day.

We had just wrapped up months of fundraising for our annual youth retreat. Only one child had consistently shown up—my god-son, Dwayne. So to honor his faithfulness, we rewarded him with a trip to the beach.

He laughed. He ran. He played.
And somewhere in the middle of his joy…
I felt sick.

Not the kind of sick that sends you running to a doctor.
Not the dramatic kind. But deep. Heavy. Spiritual.
My body was speaking. My spirit was grieving.
Something was off.

So I took a test.
Positive.

I stared at those lines, breathless—not just from fear, but from something else—
Hope.

For the first time in a long time, I saw a way out.

A baby—*my baby*—could be my exit from the prison I had been living in.

The control, the manipulation, the silence, the abuse—surely, it would all end now.

He couldn't bind me anymore because there was a child growing in my womb. I imagined freedom.

I imagined life.

But what happened next was betrayal in its most cowardly form.

He didn't offer a hand.

He didn't speak a word of prayer.

He didn't offer a plan or a promise or protection.

He insisted that I have an abortion to protect his name and ministry.

Along with that, he gave me what I had begged for before: permission to get a job.

The same man who told me I couldn't work because "God had called me to full-time ministry," suddenly released me… not out of care, but out of convenience.

Because he didn't want to be attached to this child.

So I became a greeter at Cracker Barrel.

The smell of biscuits and bacon made me nauseous.

My legs wobbled from weakness.

But I showed up anyway—every single day—because I had to.

I was working to pay for my own abortion.

When I'd saved enough, he drove me to Charlotte, North Carolina.

We pulled up in silence.

He didn't go inside.

He didn't wait.

He dropped me off… and left me alone. Terrified. Undone.

I walked inside that clinic trembling.

I was laid on a cold, sterile table. No anesthesia. No sedation.

Just a vacuum, a nurse, and a quiet voice whispering, "Breathe."

But how do you breathe when your soul is being torn apart?

They took my baby.

And with that child, they took the last untouched part of me.

The last piece I hadn't already given up to survive.

I wept—not just for the child—but for what that child represented:
My final chance to get out. My unspoken lifeline. My last yes to a
different future.

"I saw the tears of the oppressed—and they had no comforter."
—Ecclesiastes 4:1

That was me.
I cried, and no one came.
I bled, and no one stayed.
But heaven took note.

"Can a mother forget the baby at her breast? Though she may forget, I will not forget you."
—Isaiah 49:15

God saw my baby.
Even when I couldn't forgive myself, God refused to forget me.

"He heals the brokenhearted and binds up their wounds."
—Psalm 147:3

The wound of abortion is real.
But so is the healing power of grace.

I repented. I grieved. And God met me there.
He didn't just heal me. He began to restore me.

———

To the Woman Who Knows This Pain:

Maybe this is your story.

Maybe you were cornered into a choice that broke your spirit.

Manipulated. Silenced. Coerced. Pressured into silence or submission.

Hear me:

God forgives.

God restores.

And God still calls you Mother.

Your baby may not be in your arms, but they are not forgotten.

And neither are you.

———

What I Really Lost Wasn't Just a Child — It Was Time.

He didn't just rob me of a child.

He stole my youth.

I was 16 when I arrived.

Those were supposed to be my years to explore, to grow, to laugh, to love.

Instead, I was trapped.

Serving. Shrinking. Surviving.

Trying to earn love by disappearing.

He didn't just manipulate a moment—he manipulated *time*.
And suddenly, I had none left for myself.

After he died, I got married at 56.
By then, menopause had set up residence in my body.
Even if I still had the ability to have children, I no longer had the desire.

Because when you've spent decades pouring out,
the idea of starting over—even with something beautiful—can feel like a burden.

I once dreamed of lullabies, tiny feet, birthday candles, and school plays.
But now I dream of peace.

Now I dream of helping others give birth to their healing, their freedom, their next chapter.

I may not have carried a child in my womb…
But I have carried nations in my spirit.

"I will restore to you the years the locusts have eaten."
—Joel 2:25

God doesn't just restore what was lost.
He restores who you were supposed to be before the loss ever happened.

"Sing, O barren woman... for more are the children of the desolate woman than of her who has a husband."
—Isaiah 54:1

I am not barren.
I am overflowing.

I have spiritual daughters and sons.
I have legacy in books, ministries, movements.
God has made me a mother—not by biology, but by assignment.

"He settles the childless woman in her home as a happy mother of children."
—Psalm 113:9

————

Dedication: To the Woman Who Feels Forgotten

This is for the one who dreamed of cradling a baby but ended up rocking herself to sleep in grief.
This is for every womb that never stretched—but every heart that did.
For the ones who poured and parented others while no one nurtured them.
For the women told, *"You still have time,"* only to wake up with the clock striking midnight on a dream that never came true.

This is for the ones who were ready, but life wasn't.
The ones who wanted, but never got the chance.
The ones who said yes to life, and life still said no.

You are not forgotten.
You are not invisible.
You are not empty.

You are eternal.

You may not have carried a child in your womb,
but you have carried glory in your belly
and nations in your prayers.

———

Word of Release: The Grief Stops Here

To the woman grieving her lost youth,
To the one aching over an abortion she never wanted,
To the one who gave her best years to abuse, manipulation, or survival:

Let. It. Go.

Your worth is not defined by what your body didn't do.
Your calling is not cancelled because you never had children.

Your womanhood is not validated by reproduction—it is crowned by redemption.

God says:
You still have time.

Not to have what was…
But to become what's next.

Let your tears water the garden of your next season.
Let your pain become the oil that anoints your purpose.

Here is the truth:
You didn't miss it.
You *are* a mother—just not in the way the world expected.

———

The day after the abortion, the sun still rose — bold, brazen, indifferent. But I didn't. I laid there on the couch, not sleeping, not awake — just suspended. Still bleeding. Still numb. The world moved on as if nothing had happened, but inside me, everything had stopped. My body may have survived the procedure, but my soul had flatlined.

I will never forget that moment. I was on my back, the ceiling above me blurred by grief. I wasn't crying, not at first. I was empty. Hollow. Then it came — a jolt, like a lightning bolt of awareness cracking through the fog. A sudden, electric realization that the child I once carried was gone. Just… gone.

It wasn't just a thought. It was physical. Cellular. My body *knew*. My womb, which for weeks had been in protective mode — nurturing, preparing, defending — suddenly surrendered. It was like a divine switch had flipped. The feeding stopped. The guarding ceased. The sacred hush of expectancy vanished. And with it… so did I.

I pressed my hand to my stomach, where life once lived. Tears slid sideways into my ears like slow, salty confessions. "God, where are You?" I whispered.
I wanted thunder. I wanted an angel. I wanted something… anything… to interrupt the silence. But there was only breath and bleeding. And stillness.

Not absence. But silence. And there's a difference.

Then, like a thread pulled from the hem of heaven, I remembered.

A dream — one I had repeatedly since childhood — drifted into the room like a ghost.
In the dream, there was always a child. Mine, but not mine. I never saw their face. I only *felt* them. A deep knowing that I had birthed

them, that they belonged to me, and yet… they were always gone. I would wake with a strange ache, not fear, just a weight I couldn't name. Back then, I had no language. Just a lingering grief for something I never held.

But now — bleeding, broken, post-abortion — it made perfect, terrifying sense.

God had been showing me. Before I knew what abortion even was. Before I could name the detour my life would take. He knew. And in His mercy, He prepared me. That childhood dream wasn't a warning. It was a *deposit*. A down payment on future comfort. A holy foreshadowing. A preserving grace planted in my spirit before the storm ever came.

He tucked strength into the folds of my spirit while I was still innocent.

He packed a well of mercy into my marrow before I ever needed it.

He deposited hope into my shadow before I ever walked through this valley.

And lying there, soaked in my own loss, I could suddenly trace the redemptive thread.

Jesus.

From the dream I didn't understand…

To the sermons I preached about protecting children…

To the strange empathy I had, even as a little girl, for hurting women and broken mothers…

To the weight I carried for wombs and unborn souls…

It was all connected. My pain was never random. My tears were never wasted.

Some time after, the thread pulled tighter.

A man and woman came to my father. Desperate. Infertile. Shattered by doctors' reports. And my father — the same man who once told me to abort *my* child — looked at me with conviction and said, "Come here. God has given you authority to bless wombs."

I froze.

How could *he* see that in me?

How could *he*, the one who broke me, recognize what had been buried in my belly?

But he did. And God used it.

Not just prophetically. But personally. Purposefully. Painfully.

I obeyed. Still trembling. I laid hands. I spoke life. I didn't even know I carried that kind of authority. But when I did — *she conceived*. Not once, but again and again- and again. A barren woman birthed a lineage... because a broken woman dared to release what God had hidden in her.

That was the beginning.

Since then, women have found me — strangers, friends, saints and sinners alike. They'd been told they couldn't conceive. That it was over. That their wombs were dead ground. And one by one, they got pregnant. One by one, life returned.

Sometimes they rejoiced.

Sometimes they cried out, overwhelmed, "Please! Turn it off!" because the flow was *so* strong, the grace was *so* heavy, the breakthrough was *so* unstoppable.

That's when I realized...

The child I lost, God keeps giving me back.

Through others.

Through wombs I never knew I'd help unlock.

Through lives I never birthed but helped bring forth.

What I lost in the natural, He multiplied in the spirit.

He turned my miscarriage into a *mission*.

He made me a midwife of miracles.

I don't understand it fully. But I believe it deeply. I live it daily.

Because *that* dream, the one from childhood, wasn't just strange —
it was sacred. God gave me a grace before the grief, a comfort that
preceded the chaos.

We don't talk enough about that kind of grace — the *pre-installed*
kind.
The *seeded-before-the-suffering* kind.
The grace that shows up *before* we even know we'll need it.
Not just rescuing grace — but preserving grace.

And that's why I didn't lose my mind.

That's why shame didn't swallow me.

That's why bitterness didn't bury me.

Because grace was already rooted. Already ready. Already running through my blood like prophecy.

I lost a child.
But I found a mantle.
I found a mission.
I found that what the enemy tried to kill — God resurrected in me.

And now, every time I speak to a barren woman…

Every time I touch a womb in waiting…

Every time life breaks through what doctors said was dead…

I remember:
That couch.
That silence.
That jolt.
That dream.
That loss.

And I whisper, "Thank You, Jesus… for trusting me with this kind of pain. You didn't just give me grace to survive it. You gave me power to *release* it."

———

Could I Have Loved That Child?

It was the question I couldn't speak—but couldn't silence.
The question that slipped under my skin and followed me into the dark.
Could I have loved that child?
Not just in theory. Not just biologically.
But truly, deeply… righteously?

It wasn't just a thought.
It was a wrestling.
A courtroom in my soul where guilt and grace were both pleading their case.

How do you love a child whose entrance into your life came through manipulation?
How do you cradle something pure when its conception was wrapped in spiritual perversion?

Because this wasn't just about a pregnancy.
It was about the way it happened.
The confusion. The coercion.
The spiritual gaslighting dressed up as guidance.
The twisted collision between *pastor and predator, covering and captivity, anointing and abuse.*

The matter was concealed.

But God saw the war.

Even now, when I revisit that season, it makes me spiritually nauseous.
Because it wasn't just sin — it was *systemic.*
It was betrayal masked in authority.
It was "submission" weaponized against discernment.
It was a tangled web of misplaced trust and spiritual seduction.

So how was I supposed to separate that?

How was I supposed to love a child born from a moment I wished never happened?

It was unfair.
It was twisted.
It was *too much.*

And yet…
Even through the fog, even through the pain, even through the shame-soaked silence…
There it was.
A flicker.
A spark.
A sacred *knowing.*

This child had done nothing wrong.

This child was not the sin.
Not the manipulation.
Not the confusion.

This child was not a curse.
They were a soul.

And I *felt* something.

I didn't have the language for it then, but I know now — it was love.
Quiet. Raw. Unexplained.
But real.

The enemy tried to turn that love into torment.
Tried to weaponize the question against me:
Could you really love this child?
Then why did you end it?
What kind of mother are you?
What kind of woman are you?

He used it to accuse me.
To unearth my guilt.
To convince me I was unworthy —
unworthy of motherhood,
unworthy of mercy,
unworthy of healing,
unworthy of purpose.

But here's what I've learned:

God never asked us to love from our trauma.

He teaches us to love from His *truth*.

And the truth is:

Even if I didn't know how to love, the capacity was *already* in me.

Not because of the man.

Not because of the moment.

But because of God.

The situation was contaminated — but the seed was not.

The method was corrupt — but the life was sacred.

The entry point was messy — but the existence was miraculous.

That child… was known by God.

Seen by God.

Loved by God.

The Psalmist wrote:

"You knit me together in my mother's womb… All the days ordained for me were written in Your book before one of them came to be." (Psalm 139)

And I believe… somewhere deep in the hidden places of my soul

—

Yes, I did love that child.

I wept.

Even when I didn't understand what I was grieving.

I prayed.

Even when I didn't know how to form the words.

I mourned.

Because my spirit knew what my mind hadn't yet caught up to:

That love doesn't always look like fairy tales or Sunday School stories.

Sometimes love is a war cry.

Sometimes love is an ache.

Sometimes love is *lament*.

But it's love, nonetheless.

And even in the midst of confusion, corruption, and loss —

I carried a child I didn't plan for.

They discarded a child I never held.

And I loved a child I'll never forget.

Chapter 6

When the Lie Sounds Like Love

I was still reeling — body aching, spirit numb — when he said it:

"I believe you were supposed to be my wife."

The words hung in the air like incense from a strange fire — intoxicating, disorienting, and wrong.
I was mourning a child I never held. Lamenting a loss I could barely name.
And in the midst of my grief, he dressed manipulation in intimacy and called it destiny.

As if my trauma had earned me a twisted promotion.
As if spiritual abuse and heartbreak were prerequisites for an engagement ring.

Then came something darker, something sickening.

"Pray that God would take my wife."

Yes. He said that.
And for a moment — a brief, terrifying moment — I almost obeyed.

Not because I believed it was right, but because I was still searching for belonging in all the broken places.

Because the line between obedience and oppression had been blurred for so long, I couldn't see straight.

But when I opened my mouth, God intervened.

"That's witchcraft," He said. *"Don't you dare pray that. Unless you want to reap what you sow."*

It was sharp. It was clear.
A holy interruption that snatched me from the edge of spiritual ruin.

From that day forward, I warned those who prayed with me, those who still saw him as a man of God:
Don't touch that prayer. God doesn't move like that. If you ask Him to take someone out, be prepared to offer your own life in exchange. He is not a tool for your vengeance. He is not your weapon. He is holy.

Even as I spoke it, I was still unraveling inside.
I asked God about that sentence —*"You were supposed to be my wife."*
Because as warped as it sounded, part of me had wanted it to be true. I needed the pain to mean something. I needed the betrayal to have purpose.

But God showed me the truth.

"It was never love," He said. *"It was control."*
A tactic. A hook to keep me bound.
That so-called "prophetic" statement wasn't meant to reveal destiny
— it was meant to *delay deliverance.*

It wasn't divine insight. It was spiritual blackmail.

Still, even with clarity, I wasn't free.

And then, I got sick. Holding in all this corruption bankrupted my health.

The doctors diagnosed me with lymphoma cancer.
They said I had 30 days to live.

No chemo. No time.
Just prednisone and a countdown.
My body was shutting down, but my spirit was wide awake.

That diagnosis became my mirror.
It revealed not just disease, but *what was feeding it.*

And in that desperate place, God spoke again.

Not with sympathy. But with authority.

"I can't heal you if you don't forgive."

Not *I won't.*
I can't.

Healing and hatred don't flow through the same heart.

He said:

"Forgive him — for what he did to you. For the manipulation. For the abuse.
Forgive his wife — for not rescuing you, for watching it happen, for taking advantage of your silence.
Forgive the members — for seeing your suffering and doing nothing.
And forgive yourself — for being naive, for trusting too long, for staying too long, for not knowing what you couldn't have known."

It broke me.
But it also began to heal me.

I changed my diet.
I took the medication.
But more than anything, I feasted on the Word.
I confessed healing scriptures daily — not as superstition, but as medicine and survival.

Every verse was a weapon. Every confession was a rebellion against death.

"By His stripes, I am healed."

"I shall not die, but live and declare the works of the Lord."

And as I forgave — one person, one wound, one memory at a time — something shifted.

Not immediately. Not dramatically. But undeniably.

Deliverance began.

It didn't come from a service or a shout.

It came from a quiet, holy exchange between me and God —

my bitterness for His breath,

my pain for His presence,

my anger for His anointing.

That's when I understood:

Clarity is not deliverance.

Leaving the church was not deliverance.

Even rebuking manipulation was not deliverance.

Forgiveness was the door.

It was the key that unlocked healing — not just in my body, but in my soul.

And that's where the real story turns.

Not with escape. But with obedience.

Not with revenge. But with release.

Not with death. But with life — and life *more abundantly*.

And then… something happened.

One night, in the quiet of my weakness, I had a vision.

Abraham appeared to me.
Yes, Abraham, the father of faith.

He came with calm authority, like someone who had known struggle but had survived it.
And he said, "You're coming out of this. God is going to heal you. But you must do three things."

1. Always stay under authority.
2. Serve.
3. Stay obedient.

He was setting ground rules. Kingdom rules.

He knew the temptation I'd face once I got free — the urge to swing to the other extreme.
To become rebellious.
To hate every form of structure.
To reject anything that looked like leadership.

But Abraham reminded me:
True authority does exist.
God still raises up godly leaders.

Just because *this* man failed me didn't mean *every* man was corrupt.
Just because serving had once been used to trap me didn't mean I should stop serving.

"Serve with a different spirit," he said.
"Do it with love. Do it with forgiveness. Do it not because you're obligated—but because it's your calling. Never stop being a servant—because that's the posture of a true leader."

And finally: *"Obedience is better than sacrifice."*

When I awoke from that vision, I knew...

Life was about to get interesting.

Because God wasn't just healing me.
He was recommissioning me.

He was preparing me not just to survive — but to serve again.
To lead. To discern. To rebuild.
To carry truth and tenderness in the same breath.

The sickness hadn't just broken me.
It had unlocked me.

And now, I was walking out of the fire—marked, but not marred.

Delivered, not just from death…

But from the *lies* that once sounded like love.

Chapter 7

"I want my mommy!"

In just thirty days, God did what no one thought possible. The cancer—violent, invasive, and final in the eyes of medical science—vanished. Not shrunk. Not stabilized. Gone. Erased, as if heaven had reached its holy hand into my body and rewrote the narrative that death had begun to pen. The doctors stood frozen, flipping through charts like maybe they'd find the missing evidence tucked between the lines. They didn't. There was no explanation—only awe.

The testimony went viral. Kenneth Copeland Ministries picked it up and ran it like fire across the nation. But what they aired was a condensed version, I edited it and made it simplified for faith-filled consumption. It was real—but it wasn't raw. It wasn't the whole story. The depth of what I survived couldn't be reduced to five minutes of edited joy. What they didn't know—what most still don't—is that I wasn't just healed. I was haunted.

————

I was now different. Not just in body, but in soul.

I no longer behaved the way I used to. I wasn't quick to lay with him. The woman who once obeyed blindly, prayed faithfully, and gave herself fully—was now too scarred to pretend. I wouldn't risk another child. Not in this nightmare. Not under these conditions. One night, he tried to reach for me—his hand grazing my shoulder like it had so many times before—but something in me snapped. Not in anger. In agony.

I collapsed. I sobbed from a place deeper than language. All I could say was, "*I want my mommy!*"

Yes, *that* deep. That desperate. That broken. I dropped to the floor, curled into a fetal position, and held my head like it might shatter in my hands. I had watched my own mother crumble like this when life was too much, and now I was her mirror. The look on his face? Panic. Not guilt. Not compassion. Just fear. The fear of a man who had pushed too far for too long and had just met the wall he couldn't scale—me.

"I can't say anything to that," he muttered, shrinking back like a child caught red-handed. "I… I can't compete."

And just like that, he left the room.

From that moment on, the tide turned. I wasn't soft. I wasn't silent. I wasn't his anymore. And he knew it. I watched him retreat—not out of remorse, but because my resistance meant he could no longer use me. So he moved on to others.

I began seeing the same patterns—the same rehearsed compassion, the same false mentoring, the same isolated encounters. Women picked up for church alone. Women taken home after church-alone. Secret conversations. And though no one spoke it, the air itself betrayed him. You could *feel* it.

Perversion has a presence.

Sin leaves behind a spiritual scent. A residue.

Just like you feel the anointing, the Holy Spirit, or the warmth of angels—you also feel foul play. Deception. Violation. Even without proof, you *know*.

And worst of all, I saw *me* in their faces.

I had become damaged goods. Uncooperative. Guarded. And that made me useless to him. Where I was once required to go with him everywhere, now he insisted he had "things to do" on his own. One day, he casually asked if I thought someone in the ministry might be pregnant, and then he went and *bought her a pregnancy test.*

I stared at him in disbelief. *Excuse me, sir?* Why would you be the one buying her that test… unless you feared the result was connected to you?

That day, I knew. The lie that he loved me, cherished me, or protected me—shattered. I was his convenience. His concubine. Nothing more.

One weekend, I couldn't take it anymore. I packed a bag, filled up the ministry van, and drove away. I needed to escape before I imploded. A true sister in Christ opened her home and her heart to me. "Come when you need to," she said. "No permission needed." I went. But I didn't stay. Because dogs who've been caged too long won't leave even when the fence is gone.

I had been trained to remain.

And so I returned.

I wept. I prayed. I served. I remained in that invisible prison for even more years. Watched as his health declined, his body failing the way his spirit had long before. He refused doctors, rebuked my concern, and claimed my urging was an insult to his faith. Until he was too weak to argue. He would be airlifted to Greenville, then transferred to Rocky Mount. Sicker and sicker. Basins of blood. Sepsis. Hepatitis. A liver eaten alive by rot. His body became the courtroom evidence of years of sin unrepented.

But I served him until the bitter end. I brought him communion. Read faith materials aloud. Played worship music. Prayed healing over a man heaven had already judged. Because deep down, I didn't want him to die. I wanted him to change.

Chapter 8

God had issued the verdict.

It wasn't spite. It wasn't revenge. It was justice. Divine justice.

And yet, even in judgment, mercy showed up.

One Tuesday night, as he slipped between this world and the next, God brought his spirit back into his body long enough to transfer the apostolic-prophetic mantle he carried.
It was divine. Unmistakable.
A solemn, sacred transference. Not of approval—but of assignment. The baton was passed, not because he finished well, but because I had stayed faithful in the furnace.

The next morning, I called Kenneth Copeland Ministries. I asked Mr. Barry Tubbs if Papa Copeland had a word from the Lord concerning my father.

Kenneth called me directly. He said: I barely said three words to God before he interrupted with calm certainty: *"He's already home with Me."*

The final hours were brutal. The hospital bills consumed what little finances remained. There was nothing left for a funeral.

Kenneth Copeland Ministries covered every expense.

Papa Copeland said, "That's just his shell in that bed. Go make the arrangements. Send us the bill."

And just when I thought the worst was behind me—when he died, when the casket closed, and the chapter ended—something darker came to visit.

The demons that haunted him came knocking on *my* door.

It wasn't obvious at first. It wasn't theatrical. It was subtle. Seductive. Strategic. But I knew those spirits. I had seen them torment him for years. I had watched the silent war rage behind his eyes—the tension between the anointing and the addiction. The prayer and the perversion. The pulpit and the pornography.

And now, they were targeting *me*.

I started having dreams. Vivid, defiling dreams. Sexual in nature. Seductive in spirit. Dreams that made me wake up repenting and weeping because I knew—this wasn't me. This wasn't coming from within. These were *familiar spirits*. Spirits of lust. Spirits of bondage. Spirits of lawlessness. Spirits of unchecked appetite. The same spirits he gave permission to cohabitate in his life were now circling mine—looking for a door.

And they came hard.

The temptation wasn't just around me—it was *in me.* Unexplained surges of sexual desire. Random flashbacks of things I had forgotten. A curiosity toward things I had once considered vile. The algorithm of hell was trying to reprogram my spiritual DNA.

I had to fight for my purity.

Let me say this plainly: just because the mantle is clean doesn't mean the enemy won't try to drag it through mud. Satan isn't impressed by robes or titles or viral testimonies. He wants to see if you're truly set apart when nobody's watching. He'll test your "yes" in the midnight hour—when the church lights are off, when the applause has faded, when the last hospital visit is over and all that's left is your mind, your flesh, and your God.

This was deeper than temptation. It was *warfare.* And I had to contend—not just for a moment of purity, but for a *lifestyle* of it. A covenant.

I fasted. I prayed. I shut out media. I laid prostrate for hours. I cried until my pillow was soaked. I anointed my ears, my eyes, my womb, my bedroom. I read the Word aloud until my atmosphere shifted. I quoted scriptures like weapons:

"Blessed are the pure in heart, for they shall see God."

"Present your bodies a living sacrifice…"

"I made a covenant with my eyes not to look lustfully …"

I wasn't just saying "no" to sex—I was saying "no" to spirits.

No to carrying unhealed patterns into new places.
No to baptizing dysfunction and calling it grace.
No to becoming what broke me.
No to being seduced by the same thing that killed him.

Because what many people don't understand is this: mantles may come with power, but they also attract warfare. The demons that hated him now hated me. And if they couldn't destroy me the way they destroyed him, they would try to deform me—silently, sensually, secretly.

But here's the truth I had to learn the hard way:

You don't just inherit mantles. You inherit battles.

And what your predecessor didn't conquer, YOU MUST!!!
You can't skip it.
You can't shout it away.
You must SLAY IT!
OR IT WILL SLAY YOU!

So I stood my ground.

I told hell, You will not have me. You will not take what God has purified. I'm not continuing this generational mess. The contamination stops here.

I didn't just receive a mantle—I raised a standard!
The temptation was loud and my resistance was tested almost to surrender but
I refused to fall!

Not because I didn't want to. Not because it wasn't hard. Not because temptation didn't knock so loud some nights that I thought I'd crack open from the pressure. I refused because I understood the weight of my yes. The weight of leadership. The weight of my legacy, not his!

I wasn't just preserving my purity for me—I was protecting them.

The ones God had assigned to me. The sheep. The wounded. The hungry. The daughters who were coming behind me, watching how I warred in the dark. If I fell into sexual sin, they would inherit warfare they didn't sign up for. I wasn't just choosing obedience—I was building a fortress of victory for those who would follow.

That's why I told everything!
Everywhere I went, I had accountability.
I didn't hide. I didn't try to be superhuman. I confessed. I surrounded myself with godly counsel. I invited wisdom and rebuke.

I dismantled secrecy before it could settle. Because I knew: whatever I covered up would become a covering. And I didn't want any covering over me that wasn't pure.

I remember telling a mentor once, "If I give in to this—if I lay down my standard and let lust in—I won't be the only one who suffers. I'll bleed over people who came to me for healing. I'll transfer struggles to people who came to me for freedom. I'll defile the altar that God gave me to build."

I took responsibility before the fall. That's what consecration really is.

It's the refusal to trade temporary pleasure for generational torment.

I knew that if I cracked the door even slightly, the enemy would rush in—not just into my life, but into the lives of those I lead. And I loved them too much for that. I feared God too much for that. So I let the fire purify me. I let the hard seasons humble me. I let accountability break every illusion of invincibility.

Holiness wasn't just about being righteous—it was about being *safe*. Safe for God's people. Safe for the next move of God. Safe to carry glory without abusing it. Safe to stand in authority without becoming controlling, seductive, or manipulative like the man I once served under.

I had seen firsthand what happened when people carried the mantle and mishandled the people. I refused to become that.

So I stood in the gap.

I fasted to shut the mouth of lust.
I confessed when old cravings tried to revisit.
I wept when it felt like too much.
I praised when my body said give in.
I remembered the calling when the temptation screamed louder than my self-worth.

And I kept saying to myself:

> "This is not just about *me*. This is about *them*. And they're worth it."

> So I stayed pure.

And let the altar of my life say to every demon, every devil, every generational curse:

You stop here. You go no further. I may have inherited the mantle—but the demons that conquered him will not inherit me.

But even with all the accountability, the fasting, the boundaries—I hit a wall.

I remember the day I sat alone, tears streaming down my face, and I cried out to God—not in poetic tongues, not in deep intercession, but in desperation:

> "Lord, I can't focus! I'm doing ministry on autopilot. I'm preaching while perishing. I'm quoting scriptures while fighting for sanity. I'm showing up, but I'm shutting down inside. I'm struggling in my flesh. If You really want me to keep going—if You still want me to lead—I need help. Not hype. Not applause. Help!" I was honest with God and honest with the people I was leading. I solicited their prayers and covering.

And God, in His mercy, heard me.

He didn't send another platform. He didn't give me a bigger audience. He began a quiet series of *next steps*—each one designed to bring me out of survival and into deliverance… out of confusion and into clarity… out of bondage and into bridal preparation.

Each step wasn't random. They were orchestrated by the hand of a Father who knew that I had worn the mantle—but now I needed to be *healed enough* to walk in it without bleeding.

That's when the phases began.

PHASE 1: "YOU MUST GO!"

A year after his transition, I received a prophetic word—clear, loud, undeniable.

"YOU MUST GO!"

Not just physically, but spiritually, emotionally, mentally. I had outgrown the grave I was trying to worship in. The mantle didn't belong in that soil anymore.

It was exactly one year after the man of God transitioned when I received the prophetic word that marked the beginning of my exodus.

I was sitting in a service, still reeling from the silent aftershocks of nearly four decades spent under spiritual captivity. Then the word came: "You must go." That was all I needed. Heaven had spoken, and the timing was divine. However, I was trying to reconcile how was I going to walk away from the ministry I had inherited? The Lord told me to anoint and ordain my brother Robert as the Pastor.

God knew what I didn't. He knew that in order for me to truly heal, I had to leave. I couldn't be delivered in the same environment that had deceived me. I couldn't grow in the ground that had swallowed my voice. I needed distance—physical, spiritual, and emotional.

The instructions were clear: I was to go to Kenneth Copeland Bible College.

I had never planned it. It was nowhere on my radar. But shortly after that word, I found myself at the Minister's Conference hosted by Kenneth Copeland Ministries. Something in my spirit stirred. While there, I filled out the application for Bible college obeying God's instructions. I was accepted immediately.

During one of the services, the Lord whispered the exact date I was to leave North Carolina:
February 20, 2020.

Without hesitation, I texted the leaders of the church I had served so faithfully and said, *"The Lord told me to return to Bible College on February 20, 2020."*
I knew this wasn't a suggestion.
It was a divine summons.
And by the grace of God, I obeyed.

I had no idea that a global pandemic would hit just weeks later, shutting down borders, schools, and sanctuaries. But I had already crossed the line. I made it just in time.

——

A New World, A New Word

At Kenneth Copeland Bible College, I didn't just sit in a classroom—I stepped into freedom.

For the first time in my life, I was taught how to rightly divide the Word of Truth. Scriptures I had been manipulated with for years were now coming alive in context. I learned about covenant, kingdom, identity, and grace—not as tools of control but as revelations of Christ.

I had been raised in a ministry where isolation and idolatry were spiritualized. But now, God was opening my eyes to the worldview of Scripture. I had to unlearn before I could relearn. And in the process, He began healing me in ways I didn't even know I needed.

——

God's Therapy

I remember sitting in my apartment one night, tears in my eyes, wondering if I needed therapy to process it all—the trauma, the lies, the grief. Thirty-six years of spiritual captivity doesn't just dissolve in a classroom. I asked God plainly, *"Do I need to go to therapy?"*

And I will never forget what He said:
"No. I'm going to give you someone. You'll tell him what happened, and he will not say a word."

God gave me a friend at school—a young man, just a classmate. Nothing romantic, just a divine appointment. We used to study together, sit beside each other in class, laugh between lectures. And one day, God said, "*Tell him.*"

That moment changed everything.

For the first time in 36 years, I told someone what happened to me. The words that had been locked behind fear, shame, and spiritual silencing finally came out of my mouth.

And when they did, I wept.

I didn't just cry—I hollered. My body trembled. My shoulders shook. I cried from the depths of a soul that had been gagged for nearly four decades. But as I released the words, something else was released: healing.

It felt like tons were lifted from me. I was over a thousand miles away from North Carolina, but I was finally close to freedom.

That was why He sent me. Not just for biblical training—but for divine therapy. God's method. Heaven's healing.

After that, He would occasionally tell me other people I could share my story with—hand-selected listeners. Each time, it brought more healing. Little by little, my voice returned. My strength returned. My purpose became clearer.

————

Looking Back, Moving Forward

That prophetic word—"*You must go*"—was more than instruction. It was an act of mercy. It was God saying, "*I see you. I haven't forgotten you. And I will deliver you myself.*"

Kenneth Copeland Bible College wasn't just a school. It was my wilderness and my refuge, my valley and my mountaintop. It was the place where I met the God of the Bible for myself—not through manipulation, not through man-made doctrine, but through revelation, healing, and truth.

I was in Texas for two and a half years.

That was Phase One.

And though it began with departure, it birthed deliverance.

PHASE 2: The Brook Dried Up

Like Elijah at Cherith, what once fed me stopped flowing. God began closing doors, draining resources, removing people, and shifting favor. When God is done with a place, you'll know. And it's not punishment—it's preparation.

Graduation had come and gone. I had walked the stage with joy and tears, holding in my heart a deep gratitude for all that God had done. From spiritual captivity to biblical clarity, I had come a long way. I thought I was just beginning. But in God's eyes, a new chapter was already unfolding.

It started subtly.

At first, I noticed I was having trouble paying my lease. This was strange because until that moment, everything had been flowing. Bills were paid ahead of time. I was living in a beautiful luxury apartment—a place I never could have imagined living when I first left North Carolina. The hand of God had been so evident in every step.

But now... something was shifting.

———

The Seed That Opened the Floodgates

Let me take you back for a moment.

Before I even moved to Texas, before I sat in a classroom at Kenneth Copeland Bible College, I attended the Minister's Conference hosted by the ministry. During that conference, the Lord gave me an instruction that would test my faith and posture my heart for provision.

He said, "Empty your bank account. If you want to walk in over-flow, sow everything."

It wasn't a nudge. It was a command.

I didn't question it. I didn't negotiate. I obeyed.

Now here's what you need to understand: they hadn't received a single offering the entire conference. Not one. But the moment I heard God, I turned to the person who came with me and asked her to pass me an envelope. I looked at my account balance—down to the last penny—and I wrote that number on the envelope, gave my card information, sealed it, and held it in my hands like a sacred vow.

As soon as I sealed it, Jerry Savelle took the mic and said, *"We haven't received an offering this entire time, but the Lord just told me—receive an offering."*

The woman of God with me looked at me, eyes wide and mouth open. I smiled. I whispered, "I knew I heard God."

I released the seed. And God responded like only He can.

———

Provision by the Hand of God

When I returned for school, the miracles began.

On the very first day of class, I was called to the front. They handed me a check. My entire first year of Bible college had been paid in full by an anonymous donor who had seen my testimony and heard I was attending. I wept. Not just because of the money—but because God saw me.

Two weeks later, I was called to the office again.
Another check. Second year, paid in full.

Glory to God

God provided for me in every single way—housing, food, favor. I had a job working for CBN's 700 Club as a prayer counselor. It was remote. After school, I would return home, clock in, and intercede for others, even while God was healing me. I didn't lack. I didn't borrow. I didn't struggle.

Until…

———

The Shift

Graduation came, and the joy of finishing was met by the subtle discomfort of something changing.

Suddenly, the lease was hard to pay. Provision began to feel like a trickle, not a flood. I sat in my apartment one day and cried out to God:

"Lord, I don't operate in insufficiency! You told me I'd walk in overflow. Why does it feel like the brook has dried up?"

I didn't hear an answer that day.

But the next morning, I did.

———

Get Out of the House

I was asleep—just me and my little dog, Patchez—curled up, resting. And in the early morning, I heard a voice as clear as if it were standing beside me:

"Get out of the house!"

I jolted awake. My heart was racing. The urgency in the voice couldn't be ignored. It wasn't a suggestion. It was an evacuation order.

Without hesitation, I grabbed Patchez, threw on my robe, and walked out of the apartment. I walked—and walked—miles from the complex. With each step, I kept expecting to hear an explosion, see smoke, hear sirens.

But nothing happened.

I looked back.
The apartment was still standing.
Silent. Still. Intact.

Confused but obedient, I asked the Lord, "*What was that? What are you trying to show me?*"

No answer.

I walked back home. I entered the apartment and sat in the silence.

Still nothing.

———

The next morning, I poured myself a cup of coffee, sat at the dining room table, and opened my Bible. I wasn't reading long before God finally spoke.

He said,
"You asked Me why the brook dried up. I dried it."

I paused.

Then He continued,
"Your time in Texas is over. You must return home. Go back to North Carolina."

It was final. Firm. But not cruel.

I understood then—just like Elijah at the brook Cherith—God had sent me to a place of provision for a season, but now the assignment was complete. What felt like lack was really a divine signal: *It's time to move on.*

———

Return to Fayetteville

I called the youth pastor of the ministry who had always loved me well.

"Will you allow me to stay with you for a season?" I asked.

She didn't hesitate. "As long as I have a place, you have a place."

That was all I needed. I kissed Texas goodbye, and returned to Fayetteville, North Carolina—a different woman than when I had left.

———

The Lesson of the Brook

Looking back, I see it clearly now.

God didn't let the brook dry up to punish me. He let it dry up to redirect me.

When you're called to live by faith, you don't get to stay where it's comfortable. You move when He says move. You leave when He says leave. And even if the brook dries, you never forget the One who controls the flow.

Texas was my healing.
There were some loose ends that needed to be tied up in North Carolina.

And I wasn't going back as the same woman who had left under manipulation, silence, and control. I was going back with truth in my mouth, fire in my belly, and freedom in my steps. The first message I preached was "How to know you've been indoctrinated." My assignment was to free God's people from the bondage he had created all those years. I had a divine mandate to open up blinded eyes and set the captive free! I did not know to what extent until a year later but we will talk about that more in Phase 4.

PHASE 3: Solo Dates

This phase was strange and sacred. God called me to romance *my own soul*. He instructed me to take myself out. To sit alone and eat with dignity. To speak kindly to myself. To reintroduce myself to joy, presence, and stillness. I'll reveal how these solo dates weren't selfish—they were sanctified. They were dates with destiny.

When I came back to North Carolina from Texas, I thought I was returning to continue the work of ministry. I didn't realize God was about to give me an assignment for my own soul.

It started with one simple instruction:
"Go on solo dates."

At first, it didn't make sense. In Texas, I'd been laser-focused— classwork, ministry training, Bible exams, keeping an A average. There was no time to "romance myself." But here, in the stillness after my return, God was after something deeper.

I didn't understand it then, but I see it now: I wasn't ready for marriage if I wasn't comfortable in my own skin. I couldn't truly love someone else if I hadn't learned how to enjoy my own company.

From Fayetteville to Wilson

When I first came back, I stayed in Fayetteville. But my church was in Wilson, North Carolina. Every weekend, I packed up my things, carried them down three flights of stairs, drove an hour and a half to stay with the wife of my spiritual father—the woman I'd grown up calling "Mother." Then Monday would come, and I'd pack it all back up, haul it back up those same stairs, and do it again the next weekend.

Six months of that wore me out.

One day, driving back from Wilson, I sighed and said aloud, "Lord, I'm tired of this."
And in my heart, I knew: *I'd rather be in Wilson full time.*

So I moved into the church building itself. No bedroom. No kitchen. Just space on the floor for me to lay my head. I'd go back and forth to "Mother's" house to shower, iron clothes, and prepare for services. It wasn't glamorous, but it was obedience.

The First Solo Date

Somewhere in that final six months in Wilson, God said,

"It's time to start."

So I got dressed and went to an upscale restaurant—alone.

The moment I sat down, I felt it: awkward. Every table seemed filled with couples leaning into each other, laughing, "boo'd up" as we say. And there I was—just me, my menu, and the Lord.

I wanted to leave. But I stayed. I ate. I paid the bill. I went home.

The next Friday night, I did it again. Different place, same awkward feeling. But little by little, week by week, I stopped noticing the couples and started noticing me.

Fridays became my night. Bowling. The movies. The park. Sometimes a burger and fries, sometimes fine dining. It wasn't about what I did—it was about being intentional with myself. About saying: *You're worth time. You're worth investment. You're worth joy.*

———

The Breakthrough

One Friday, I chose a seafood restaurant. I ordered a full seafood boil—crab legs, potatoes, corn on the cob, sausage, all seasoned to perfection in one of those big steam bags. I ordered a special drink, set my iPad on the table, picked a good movie, and dug in.

And for the first time, I didn't feel alone. I felt **content**.

When I finished, I had them bag up my leftovers. I stood, walked out into the night air, and in that moment the Lord spoke:

"Congratulations. Your season of singlehood is over."

I froze. Tears sprang to my eyes. I lifted my hands right there in the parking lot and praised Him. Something had shifted.

God had done something in me that no man could take credit for— I was whole.

———

Olive Garden and a Revival

The following Friday, my sister Lisa rode with me. I laughed and told her, "You know, I don't have to do this alone anymore. My solo season is over. Where do you want to go?"

She picked Olive Garden.

As we pulled into the parking lot, the Lord spoke again:
"Invite an apostle to come and preach revival at your church."

I told Lisa, "The Lord just gave me an instruction. I'm going to call him now." I called and said, "The Lord told me to invite you for revival." He said he'd check his schedule and call back. Before long, he confirmed: "I'll be there next weekend."

When he came, he preached powerfully the first night. As was our custom, we covered his hotel and one meal per day while he was with us, and we gave him 50% of the offering. The next day, I asked where he wanted to eat, and invited my internet pastor to join us.

———

The Question Over Lunch

Over lunch, because he was on my board of accountability, I updated him on the ministry:
"The people are adjusting to the new order of Kingdom living," I said. "But I only take one issue with God."

He smiled. "What's that?"

I looked him straight in the eye.
"Where is my husband?"

He chuckled, then said something that caught me off guard:
"There's a man of God who used to be in my ministry—he's been believing God for you."

I leaned back. "What?"

He described him—a man of integrity, someone I remembered as kind and respectable. I then told that apostle: "Tell him I said call me!" He kind of agreed and the conversation went on to other things.

When lunch ended, I climbed into my car, still thinking about it. That's when the Lord said:

"He's not going to tell him. If you want to close this gap, call your mutual friend."

———

The Connection

I didn't hesitate. I called her.

Immediately, she began to share: "Do you know he's been believing God for you ever since he saw your transformation on Facebook?"

That made me smile. Because my "transformation" had been God's doing. I'd been raised in a rigid, religious environment—no makeup, no earrings, no pants, only oversized dresses to hide my figure. But before I flew to Texas, the Lord told me,

"When you get there, I don't want you to look anything like what you came out of. Your husband will find you in Texas."

I assumed He meant my husband would *be* from Texas. But God didn't say that—He said my husband would *find* me in Texas.

In Texas, the Lord told me to post my transformation photos online. I thought it was for people in bondage—to show them you could be free and still be anointed. And maybe it was. But it was also so my husband could see me.

He wasn't on social media at all. But our mutual friend was. One day she asked him, "Have you seen LaShea lately?" When he said no, she showed him a photo. The second photo she showed him, he declared:

"That's my wife!"

A Word to My Single Sisters: Your Single Season Is Sacred

Ladies, let me tell you something—your single season is not a punishment. It's not a delay. It's a **strategic season of preparation** where God is doing deep, foundational work in you that will bless you for the rest of your life.

We live in a world where "single" is often treated like a waiting room—like life hasn't really started yet until you have a ring on your finger. But I'm here to declare to you: **Your single season is not a pause button. It's a purpose season.**

―――

1. Solo Dates Are Not Selfish — They're Strategic

When God told me to start going on solo dates, I didn't understand it. I thought, *What is this? Why is this important?* But I learned something powerful: If you can't enjoy your own company, you won't know how to steward someone else's.

The Word says in **Mark 12:31**:

> "Love your neighbor as yourself."

> We quote that a lot, but here's the truth—if you don't know how to love *yourself*, you will not be able to love anyone else well.

> Solo dates teach you to value yourself, to invest in yourself, to see yourself the way God sees you. It's not about spending money—it's about sending a message to your own soul:

I am worth time. I am worth joy. I am worth being treated with honor.

―――

2. Your Relationship with God in This Season Is Vital

Ladies, your single season is the perfect time to go deeper with God. Paul said it best in **1 Corinthians 7:34**:

"An unmarried woman or virgin is concerned about the Lord's affairs: Her aim is to be devoted to the Lord in both body and spirit."

When you're single, you have a kind of freedom you won't always have in marriage—you can pour all of yourself into knowing Him, hearing Him, and obeying Him without divided attention.

And hear me: **God is strategic.**
When you walk with Him closely in this season, He will order your steps so precisely that you will not only be delivered from your past—you will be positioned for your future.

———

3. God Can Bring You Out and Into

I know what it is to be bound—to be captivated by manipulation, crushed by abandonment, and shackled by despair. But I also know the God who delivers.

Psalm 40:2 says:

"He lifted me out of the slimy pit, out of the mud and mire;

He set my feet on a rock and gave me a firm place to stand."

God is not just in the business of bringing you *out*—He's in the business of bringing you *into*.

From captivity to calling.

From heartbreak to healing.

From despair to destiny.

———

4. Obedience Is Your Key to Destiny

Every step of my journey from captivity to freedom was tied to obedience.

- **"Go to Texas."** I went.
- **"Start solo dates."** I did it, even when it felt awkward.
- **"Invite that apostle."** I obeyed, and it opened a door.

Jesus said in **John 14:15**, *"If you love Me, keep My commandments."* When you love God enough to obey Him—even when it doesn't make sense—you set yourself up for divine appointments that no man can orchestrate.

———

5. Deliverance Comes Before Destiny

Before God introduced me to my husband, He introduced me to *me.*

He healed the little girl in me who had been overlooked.
He set free the woman in me who had been silenced.
He restored the leader in me who had been diminished.

Why? Because God doesn't just give you a spouse—He gives you *wholeness.*

And He knows you can't truly partner in destiny if you're still bleeding from the wounds of captivity.

To Every Single Woman Reading This

Sis, I need you to hear me in the Holy Ghost: This season is holy. Don't rush it. Don't despise it. Don't waste it.

If you will let Him, God will:
- Heal the parts of you no one else sees.
- Restore the joy the enemy tried to steal.
- Train your ears to recognize His voice.
- Position you so that when your destiny meets you, you'll be ready to embrace it fully.

Psalm 37:4 says:

"Delight yourself in the LORD, and He will give you the desires of your heart."

Delight in Him first. Let Him romance you. Let Him teach you your worth. Let Him prepare you—not just for marriage, but for your *mission.*

And when the time is right, the same God who brought me from 36 years of captivity into freedom, purpose, and love will do the same for you.

Stay faithful. Stay obedient. Stay ready.
Your destiny is closer than you think.

PHASE 4: Where Is My Husband?

The cry for companionship got louder. Not from desperation, but readiness. After all I'd endured, I wanted to know: *Where is he, Lord?* Did my obedience cost me love? Did my pain disqualify me from partnership?

I didn't hesitate.

When I called our mutual friend, I told her what I'd heard. She laughed. "Oh, he likes you, alright." Then she paused. "Wait—are you interested?"

"Yes," I said without blinking.

She nearly squealed. "Okay, let me call him. I'll tell him you said you won't go to bed tonight until he calls you."

She tried him once—no answer. Twice—still no answer. Finally, on the third try, he picked up. She told him, "Your confession has manifested. LaShea says she won't go to bed tonight until you call her."

About an hour later, my phone lit up with a South Carolina number. He was in the middle of dropping off his last load from his old house before moving into his new home in Augusta, Georgia.

I answered with a smile in my voice. "Earl, I didn't know you liked me."

His first words: "*LaShea McKinney, if this is a dream, don't wake me up.*"

———

We talked for nearly an hour. He told me he had liked me from the beginning, years ago.

"I watched you," he said. "You were focused. You served in ministry. You weren't flirtatious. You were dedicated. And every time y'all came to revival at my former pastor's church, they'd put you in a house where you cooked for the ministers. One night I tasted your cooking, and I thought, *She'd make a good wife.*

"But when I saw your picture on Facebook after all those years, I said to our friend, *She's free. Look at her.* You looked so happy. I knew Apostle McKinney was probably turning over in his grave, but you looked free. It was something about that picture—it showed your heart. I could see you had come into your own. You weren't bound by religion anymore. You were enjoying life. You were loving yourself. And I fell in love with you.

"I asked our friend for another picture of you, and I put it on my phone wallpaper. For three and a half years, every morning, I looked at that picture and prayed, *Lord, give her to me to be my wife.* I never called you. I never reached out. I wanted God to do it without my flesh touching it.

"Women would ask me who that was on my phone. I told them, *That's my wife.* Every morning, I'd pick up my phone, kiss your picture, and say, *Good morning, wife.* And then I'd thank God for you."

———

I want to pause here and speak to every single woman reading this.

Prophetic Romance Reflection – God Still Writes Love Stories

Your husband is not lost. He's not late. And you don't have to chase him. The same God who authored marriage is the same God who can orchestrate yours.

When I boarded that plane to Texas, God told me, *"When you get there, I don't want you to look anything like what you came out of. Your husband will find you in Texas."* I assumed He meant my husband would be *in* Texas. But He didn't say that.

Be careful how you hear.

God took me to Texas to deliver me, heal me, and set me free—not just for ministry, but for marriage. While I was walking out my obedience in Texas, a man in South Carolina was praying for me daily, without me knowing, trusting God to bring us together.

The Bible says:
- *"Delight yourself in the LORD, and He will give you the desires of your heart."* – Psalm 37:4
- *"No good thing will He withhold from those who walk uprightly."* – Psalm 84:11
- *"The steps of a good man are ordered by the LORD, and He delights in his way."* – Psalm 37:23

Your role is not to make it happen—it's to walk closely with God until it happens.

And that walk? It's not passive. It's about becoming:

- Becoming healed from past wounds.
- Becoming confident in your own skin.
- Becoming a woman who knows her worth and won't settle.
- Becoming so consumed with God's purpose that marriage is a blessing, not a rescue plan.

If God could do this for me—after thirty-six years of captivity, after decades of manipulation and pain—He can do it for you.

Beloved, you don't have to manipulate a connection or rush God's timeline. Stay the course. Stay in His presence. And when He says *Now*, your love story will be more than romance—it will be prophecy fulfilled.

———————

When we got ready to get off that very first phone call, I told him, "You have my number—use it. And from now on, every conversation we have, I want you to end it in prayer."

That request wasn't casual. I wanted to hear the depth of his relationship with God. I had already seen his faith—faith was what made me fall in love with him before I even knew I loved him. After years of being mishandled, abandoned, and dropped, here was a man who had literally prayed for me, who had gone to God and asked Him for me.

You have to understand how rare that is for a woman who had never truly belonged to anyone who loved her enough to seek Heaven on her behalf. He didn't win my heart with money. He didn't win my heart with charm. He won it because he desired God's will more than his own and stayed celibate, prayed, and waited for me. That alone commanded my attention.

His faith moved me the way faith moves God.

"Without faith it is impossible to please Him." – Hebrews 11:6
If faith moves God—and I am God's daughter—then faith was going to move me, too.

So we talked. For two weeks, we spoke daily, sometimes for hours. Each conversation ended in
prayer, just as I had asked. We laughed. We shared stories. We prayed over each other.

On the third conversation, as we were saying goodbye, the words slipped out before I even knew they were coming:
"I love you."

We hung up, and a second later, I texted him: Did I just say 'I love you'?

"Yes, you did," he replied. "And I was shocked… but pleasantly."

I realized then—his faith had already captured my heart.

———

Two weeks later, I woke up with a knowing in my spirit: *I'm supposed to be where he is.*

We had chemistry on the phone, but I needed to know if it was the same in person—could we breathe the same air and still feel at home? Would I be at ease? Would it feel like destiny?

I called our mutual friend. "I think I'm supposed to be there," I told her.

She didn't hesitate. "Shea, I feel the same. They just finished decorating the house. I think you should come."

Here's the thing—after all those years of being mishandled, I would never have gone to a man's city alone. But God had orchestrated it so that one of my covenant partners from ministry lived right there in Augusta, Georgia. That made me feel safe. It was His divine way of removing every excuse I might have had not to go.

———

At the time, I was working for one of my own church members. She had been there through all my seasons of praying for my husband. She had heard me stand in the pulpit and say, "I sense my husband. I feel he's nearby. Our paths are about to cross." That was long before I even knew who he was.

So when I told her, "I've met someone, and I'm thinking about going to visit," she smiled and said, "Move in silence. Don't tell anyone. If God told you to do it, go. You have my blessing, and your job will be here when you get back."

I packed my things, drove to Augusta… and never came back.

———

From the start, I knew I couldn't build a marriage on pretense. The very first thing I did when I saw him in person was pour out my story—all of it. Every scar. Every wound. Every betrayal. I knew that if he could still want me after knowing the truth, then this was something God had truly ordained.

I told him things that broke my own heart to say out loud. We cried together. He prayed over me.

He was stunned—not because he doubted me, but because he had loved and respected Apostle McKinney so deeply. "I can't believe he did this to you," he said, shaking his head. But he knew I was telling the truth. There were too many details, too much rawness, too much Spirit in the telling for it to be fabricated.

When I finished, he took my hands and said, "Well, since you told me your life… let me tell you mine."

His Prison

He told me, "When I was seven or eight years old, my mother was with a man she later married. The two of them poisoned my father. They killed him."
From that moment, his life was changed.

He and his siblings were locked in a room every night.
No freedom to walk through the house.
No kitchen to raid when hunger struck.
No joy of a holiday morning.
Just beans and rice—maybe a chicken back if they were lucky.

Each of them received compensation checks after their father's death. They never saw a dime. The money was taken, and they went without Christmas.
The only gifts came from their grandmother—small bags with one or two pairs of socks.

By the time he was a teenager, he was working—mowing yards, doing anything to buy his own school clothes.

At sixteen, he moved out and got his own place.

But trouble found him anyway.

———

False Accusations

First came the milk truck incident.

He was walking with his cousin when his cousin—without warning—jumped on a milk truck, pulled a gun, and robbed the driver.

Earl didn't know a thing about it until it happened.

He hid behind the truck as shots rang out, waiting until every bullet was fired before he ran.

But people saw him run.

They told police.

And the next thing he knew, the police were at his house.

Though he had no part in the crime, he was sent to prison—for four years.

The second time came when he was in the wrong place again.

A man he knew went into a restaurant-bar, told Earl what he planned to do, and Earl said no.

But he stayed on the premises.

The man went inside, locked people in a room, robbed the place, and came out with the money.

Earl got in the car with him, not knowing what had just happened.

Before long, police spotted them.

A high-speed chase began.

Gunshots were exchanged.

By the time they were caught, the law tied Earl to the crime.

This time, it cost him 17 years of his life.

————

Love, Disappointment, and Loss

In prison, a friend introduced him to a woman—a musician in the church.

They talked on the phone.

She visited.

She seemed like a Christian.

They became close, and in a moment of weakness, he crossed a line.

Wanting to make it right before God, he married her.

But when he was released, he discovered she wasn't the woman of God he thought she was.

She didn't like his deep commitment to holiness.

After a year, the marriage ended in divorce.

She passed away some years later.

————

Our Mirrored Stories

When Earl finished, I realized we were the same in so many ways.

I had been in an emotional and spiritual prison.

He had been in a physical one.

We had both been mishandled by those who should have loved us.

We had both been accused of things we didn't do.

We had both been abandoned.

But here we were—two freed prisoners—facing each other.

Not because of luck.

Because of God's strategy.

God's Orchestration

While I was being healed from my prison of spiritual abuse,

God was forming him in a prison of steel and bars.

While I was learning to walk in freedom,

he was learning to wait in faith.

Two swords, sharpened in different furnaces, forged to fight together.

When we said "I do," it wasn't just a wedding.

It was a prophetic act.

Two stories of captivity joining in covenant freedom.

Two weeks after that first call, I was here.

And in **38 days**, we were married.

Thirty-eight days.
After thirty-six years of heartbreak, delay, and captivity, God exchanged the years with days—days filled with His orchestration, His timing, His glory.

We didn't need a long courtship.
We knew.
We *knew*.

So in a private ceremony, we became husband and wife.
Not because we were in a rush, but because we were in obedience.
Not because we were desperate, but because we were destiny.

———

God took two prisoners—one of steel bars and one of spiritual chains—
and set us free *together*.
He proved that He can accelerate what you thought would take a lifetime.
He showed that He will redeem the years the locusts have eaten (Joel 2:25).
And He whispered to both of us, *"This is the one you prayed for."*

AFTER MARRIAGE — THE FINAL YES

After 38 days, I became Mrs. Hunter. God had turned my 36 years into 38 days, bringing me into the promise I had waited on my entire life. But marriage didn't mean the testing was over—it meant a new chapter of obedience had begun.

Shortly after we married, I had to return to North Carolina to preach at my church for Apostle's Day, the fifth Sunday service. My brother was pastoring, and I was the apostle.

When I walked into the sanctuary, the air was heavy. I felt it instantly—the spirit of death. I said nothing to anyone, but I knew it was there. After the message, while I was changing in the study, the Lord spoke clearly:

> "This church is on life support. It is dying. You will have to pull the plug."

In that moment, I remembered Apostle McKinney's words before he died:

> "When I die, my vision will die, and God will give you your own."

He had known his works would not remain—that his legacy would not stand in the eyes of God.

I left that day in a storm of thoughts. All my life I had been taught how to plant, how to endure, how to rebuild—but never how to close down a church. The weight of those few remaining members pressed on me. Would they scatter? Would their blood be on my hands? Was this truly God or my own weariness speaking?

When I shared it with my husband, I was in tears. For weeks—months—I wrestled. My husband, however, understood immediately. To him, it was God's final closure on a painful chapter. He hugged me, but his stance was steady: this was God, not loss.

Still, I felt untethered. For 36 years, shepherding had been my anchor. Without a congregation, who was I? What was my role? What did an apostle without a church even look like?

In the meantime, I attended the church my husband was loyal to. It was familiar—but not in a good way. The same hierarchical control. The same "star" leader mentality. Once you've been in it, you can smell it in the air.

The pastor noticed my gifts and began to ask me to minister. Eventually, he offered me a position as his administrator, matching my salary from my job at Cato's. I agreed to consider it for my husband's sake—but the Lord told me to draft a written contract. The pastor refused to sign it. That was my answer.

God's voice was clear:

"I didn't bring you together to build someone else's empire. You were forged in fire to set multitudes free."

I had already resigned from my job to take the church position, so I had to swallow my pride and return to Cato's—only to find my role given away, returning for less pay.

But God was working. My husband began to see what I had seen all along. One morning, after prayer, he realized that his pastor already expected my husband to leave when he married me.

Days passed in silence. My husband wept, wrestling with loyalty. Then he said the words that broke us both:

"Now I know how you felt when you had to close your church. This was the only church family I've known for 13 years."

And just like that, we were in agreement. We drafted a resignation letter and left.

For the next year and a half, we were shut in—fasting, praying, healing, and saying a complete yes to God. That "yes" included the one thing I didn't want to do—write this book.

I told the Lord I wanted to move on quietly, but He said, "If you don't write it, everything you went through was for nothing." My spiritual father confirmed it.

So here it is—Faith Unchained. My testimony of escaping the snare of a misleading spiritual leader. My story of being healed, restored, and rebuilt.

If these pages find you in the grip of manipulation, control, or spiritual abuse, I pray you find the courage to get an exit strategy.

Get out.
Your life depends on it.

Appendix — Breaking Free: A Handbook for Pastor's Wives and the Spiritually Trapped

To Pastor's Wives Who Suffer in Silence

I did not mention much about Apostle McKinney's wife in this book—not because her story wasn't important, but because this was *my* testimony. Still, I cannot close without addressing a group of women who are often the first casualties of toxic ministry culture: the wives of pastors, apostles, and leaders in hierarchical, prophetic, or charismatic churches where the "man of God" operates unchecked.

Before the sheep are manipulated, the shepherd's wife is often the **first victim**.

You know the late-night "appointments," the solo trips, the locked office doors.
You smile for the church cameras but sleep in a separate bed.
You counsel women but cry yourself to sleep.
You protect the image while losing yourself.

God never intended for you to be a **prop for someone else's pulpit**.

Proverbs 31:25 —*"She is clothed with strength and dignity; she can laugh at the days to come."*

Remaining silent to protect an image gives sin room to grow and robs you of your God-given dignity.

My Plea to You:

1. **Be brutally honest with God.** He already knows, but honesty opens the door to His direction.

2. **Count the cost of staying AND leaving.** Staying can cost your soul, health, and children's future.

3. **Seek counsel outside your ministry.** *Proverbs 11:14 —"In the multitude of counselors there is safety."*

4. **Know the difference between loyalty and bondage.** Loyalty never requires protecting evil.

5. **Plan your exit in wisdom.** If God releases you, prepare spiritually, emotionally, financially, and practically.

———

Part 2 — For Anyone in a Cult-like or Abusive Church System

Leaving an abusive ministry is not just "walking away." They use fear, scripture twisting, and false prophecy to make you believe leaving is betraying God.

> **Galatians 5:1** —*"It is for freedom that Christ has set us free. Stand firm... and do not be burdened again by a yoke of slavery."*

Step-by-Step Exit Plan

Step 1 — Pray for Clear Direction
- Ask God for undeniable confirmation from His Word.
- Scriptures: Psalm 34:17–18, Isaiah 61:1–3, John 8:32, Jeremiah 29:11.
- Journal what you sense; God often repeats Himself for clarity.

Step 2 — Recognize the Red Flags
You may be in spiritual bondage if:
- Questioning leadership is seen as rebellion.
- You are shamed for seeking counsel outside the ministry.
- Finances are manipulated with heavy pressure to give.
- The leader has no accountability.
- Secrecy and favoritism are common.

Step 3 — Build Support Outside
- Confide in at least one safe, Spirit-filled person outside the ministry.
- *Hebrews 10:24–25* reminds us to keep godly fellowship, not toxic fellowship.

Step 4 — Make a Practical Exit Plan
- Secure housing if you live in ministry property.
- Start saving money discreetly.
- Collect important documents now.

Step 5 — Break Points of Control
- Leave group chats, mailing lists, and ministry social media.

- Change your number or block harassing contacts.

Step 6 — Heal Before You Rebuild
- Don't rush to another church.
- Seek counseling from someone trained in spiritual abuse recovery.
- Refuse false guilt—leaving an abusive church is not leaving Christ.

———

Scriptures to Stand On
- **Psalm 18:2** — *"The LORD is my rock, my fortress and my deliverer."*
- **Isaiah 41:10** — *"Fear not, for I am with you… I will strengthen you."*
- **2 Corinthians 3:17** — *"Where the Spirit of the Lord is, there is freedom."*
- **Psalm 147:3** — *"He heals the brokenhearted and binds up their wounds."*

———

Practical Resources
- **Spiritual Abuse Recovery Resources** — www.spiritualabuse.org
- **Hope Again Recovery** — Support for those leaving high-control churches.
- **FaithTrust Institute** — www.faithtrustinstitute.org

- **National Domestic Violence Hotline** — 1-800-799-SAFE (7233)

———

Part 3 — Kingdom Forge International™

My husband and I founded Kingdom Forge International™ because we have walked through both spiritual and natural imprisonment. We were forged in fire, betrayed, stripped, and rebuilt by God's hand.

Our mission is to:
- Break chains.
- Restore the broken.
- Equip the silenced to speak.

We are not a church; we are a Kingdom deliverance and equipping ministry.

Email: kingdomforgeintl@gmail.com

If you need prayer, counsel, or help finding a safe way out of a toxic ministry, reach out. You are not alone.

John 8:36 — *"So if the Son sets you free, you will be free indeed."*

Father, I thank You for every person reading this. Right now, break every chain that holds them. Silence the voice of fear and open the path of freedom. Heal the wounds of betrayal. Restore their joy, renew their faith, and lead them beside still waters. In Jesus' name, amen.

——

Chapter X – To My Critics

You will read my story and some of you will sit in awe, wondering how I endured so much.

Others will read and shake your head, saying:

- "Why didn't you just leave?"
- "You were grown — you could have gotten out."
- "How could you live in the same house with the woman you called your mother and still allow her husband to force himself into your bed?"
- "Why share this? Doesn't it hurt the Church?"

Before you decide who I was or what I should have done, let me speak plainly.

——

"Why didn't you just leave?"

Leaving isn't always about finding a door — sometimes it's about finding the strength to believe you deserve to walk through it. Abuse, especially spiritual abuse, doesn't just trap your body — it traps your mind, your sense of worth, and your picture of God. I wasn't just in a house; I was in a belief system. My loyalty, my identity, and my calling were all tied to the place and man who was harming me. It's hard to walk away when you've been taught that walking away from them is walking away from God. And when all other family was taken away from you- you would be surprised how you can be conditioned to normalize toxicity. I literally knew these people longer than I knew my biological family.

————

"You were grown — why did you allow it?"

I was grown, but I was also groomed- groomed from age 16 to 52. Grooming doesn't end at childhood — it can happen to anyone whose trust is manipulated and whose environment is controlled. My adulthood didn't make me immune to deception; it only made me a more useful servant in the eyes of my abuser. I had been conditioned to believe that enduring was part of my spiritual assignment.

————

Living in that house

You want to know how I could still live under the same roof with the woman I called my mother while her husband violated me. I'll tell you — because that question haunts me too.

I loved her. I truly did. She was the closest thing to a mother I had known after my biological mother put me out. I wanted her to be loved and cherished by her husband so badly that I tried to help her be more appealing to him. I bought her clothes. I sewed for her with my own hands. I brought her perfumes, bath oils, and lingerie. I encouraged her in her beauty, hoping he would turn back toward her and leave me the heck alone.

But he didn't want her. He wanted control. He wanted power. And I became the scapegoat for what she could not stop or would not see. I carried guilt that wasn't mine, trying to fix a marriage I didn't break, while silently enduring a violation I never chose.

I could still call her my mother because I wanted to believe she loved me, because hope was the last thread holding my heart together. But my loyalty also kept me bound. I didn't yet understand that love without boundaries becomes a chain.

"How could you, a woman of God, not see what was happening?"

Because wolves don't come with fangs showing — they come wearing shepherd's clothes. I saw a man who was truly anointed, a leader I trusted, a spiritual father figure. I confused charisma for character. I missed the signs because the evil was dressed in Scripture and prophecy and when it dawned on me, I tried to leave an

162

innumerable number of times but I had no where to go for fear of someone worse in my vulnerability taken further advantage of me. I was conditioned.

———

"Why share all this publicly? Doesn't it damage the Church?"

What damages the Church is not my testimony — it's the abuse that birthed it. Silence is what rots the Body from the inside out. The only way to protect God's people is to expose what hides in His house. My story is not meant to tear down the Church; it is meant to cleanse it. Light never destroys what is pure — it only reveals what was already corrupt.

———

"Why didn't you speak up sooner?"

Because in a culture of control, the one who speaks up is made to be the problem. I feared losing the only community I had left, the ministry I had sacrificed for, and the spiritual covering I was told I could not live without. Speaking up required me to unlearn fear, rebuild courage, and trust God to hold me if man rejected me again. Healing taught me that what I suffered and won was not only for me but for millions of others who would come after me.

———

"Do you still blame them?"

I don't live in blame — I live in truth. Forgiveness freed me from revenge, but truth freed me from their narrative. I can forgive without pretending it never happened. I can move forward without protecting the image of the one who harmed me.

———

"Aren't you afraid people will think less of you?"

I'm more afraid of God thinking less of me if I bury the truth He told me to tell. My reputation is in His hands. If my honesty costs me human approval, then that is a price I'm willing to pay for someone else's deliverance.

———

To the critic who says, *"That could never be me"* — I pray it never is.
Because when abuse wears the mask of family, faith, and false safety, you don't just walk away.
First, you have to realize these kind of chains aren't made of metal and the invisible ones seem to keep you the longest and grip you the tightest.

———

Prayer for the Critics

Father, I lift before You every heart and every mind that will read these words.

For those who come with curiosity, grant them clarity.

For those who come with criticism, grant them compassion.

Lord, remove from them the pride that says, "*It could never be me,*" and replace it with the humility that says, "*God, keep me.*"

Open their eyes to the subtle chains that can bind a soul — chains made not of metal, but of manipulation, misplaced loyalty, and misunderstood Scripture.

I pray that the same mercy You extended to me in my darkest hours would meet them in theirs, should they ever find themselves trapped in a place they swore they'd never be.

Shield them from the predators that grace pulpits, the false prophets that twist Your Word, and the spiritual leaders who confuse control with care.

And for every critic who has been secretly carrying their own story — hiding it because of shame, fear, or the judgment of others — I speak freedom now in the name of Jesus.

May Your truth be their deliverance.

May Your Spirit be their guide.

May Your love be their refuge.

Lord, I release every critic into Your hands.

Transform them from spectators into intercessors, from doubters into defenders, and from those who question my survival into those who help others survive.

In Jesus' name,
Amen.

——

A Letter to My Mother and to My Siblings

Dear Mom,

You left this world in 2017, just a year before the one who held me captive passed away. In all those years, I never had the chance to say these words to you face-to-face, so I write them now with the hope that heaven allows you to hear the cries of my heart.

That day you put me out, I know you believed you were protecting me. You saw danger, and out of fear you thought pushing me away would somehow save me. But instead of covering me, I was delivered into a captivity that lasted 36 years. I know now that you weren't equipped with the tools or the wisdom to handle it differently. You did what you thought was best, even if it caused me deep pain. I believe you acted out of fear, not out of hatred. And while I carried that wound for so long, today I want to say: I forgive you. I understand your intent, even if the outcome was devastating.

To my siblings—I missed so much of your lives. When I left, you were just children. My sister was only about six, my brother just a little younger. I never wanted to miss your birthdays, your milestones, or the moments that bond siblings together. It wasn't my choice to be absent; I was told I could have no more contact with you. Mom was afraid the danger I was in might reach you too, so I obeyed her request even though it broke me inside. Please know—it was never rejection. It was never my lack of love. It was obedience to what I was asked, even though it cost me the joy of walking beside you.

And to my younger sisters—those I never got to know, born after my path had already been set—I want you to know that even though we never shared childhood memories, I still carry you in my heart. You are part of me, and I honor your place in this family. My absence in your lives was never by choice, but by circumstance. I love you, too.

To all of you, my brothers and sisters: I never stopped being your sister in my heart. I never stopped loving you. My deepest prayer is that the years the enemy stole will be redeemed by love, grace, and restoration.

With all my love,
LaShea

www.ingramcontent.com/pod-product-compliance
Lightning Source LLC
Chambersburg PA
CBHW050405030726
47503CB00006B/2031